"Where do we eat?" Hannah asked

"Wherever you like, Hannah," Khalil said softly. "Outside in the garden, beneath the sky stitched with stars—"

She interrupted him, her senses alerted by the velvet tones of his voice. "To hell with your embroidery. This is a restaurant, isn't it?" she asked warily.

"No, it's my house. I'm glad you like it," he said lazily.

He sounded like a wolf about to devour a fat lamb, Hannah thought. And it was she who was up for slaughter. How stupid to walk into his lair. She stared back at him, nerves rendering her momentarily speechless.

"Why bring me here?" she managed to say at last.

"To seduce you, of course," he drawled.

SARA WOOD lives in a rambling, sixteenth-century home in the medieval town of Lewes amid the Sussex hills. Her sons have claimed the cellar for bikes, making ferret cages, taxidermy and wine making, while Sara has virtually taken over the study with her reference books, word processor and what have you. Her amiable, tolerant husband, she says, squeezes in wherever he finds room. After having tried many careers—secretary, guest-house proprietor, play-group owner and primary teacher—she now finds writing romance novels gives her enormous pleasure.

Books by Sara Wood

HARLEQUIN PRESENTS

HARLEQUIN ROMANCE

SARA WOOD

nights of destiny

Harlequin Books

TORONTO • NEW YORK • LONDON
AMSTERDAM • PARIS • SYDNEY • HAMBURG
STOCKHOLM • ATHENS • TOKYO • MILAN

To Abdellalif and Heather,
with grateful thanks for
their Marrakshi welcome and hospitality.

Harlequin Presents first edition July 1991
ISBN 0-373-11382-X

Original hardcover edition published in 1990
by Mills & Boon Limited

NIGHTS OF DESTINY

CHAPTER ONE

HANNAH burst into the warehouse like an exploding bomb, dazzling the eyes with her electric-blue suit and trailing saffron scarf. The large building crawled with workmen, and with one accord they downed tools to watch her as she strode vigorously across the partially tiled floor, her wide shoulders swaying, her whole body a series of seductive motions, hampered slightly by the tight, short skirt.

'Hello, everyone!' she cried enthusiastically. 'Frankie!' she yelled at a quiet, bespectacled woman who was perched dangerously on some scaffolding. 'Guess where I'm going to live?'

Frankie grinned and waved, but Hannah was too excited to wait for her to come down. The workmen awaited developments, fascinated by Hannah's vibrancy this morning. It seemed that even the strands of her tumbling blonde hair were alive, the way they danced on her shoulders. Impatiently, she planted her hands on the firm swell of her hips.

'I've rented a house in an orange grove.' Hannah paused theatrically, for effect. *'On the Casablanca Road!'*

Frankie paused, too, still a few feet from the ground, and turned to stare in awe. Hannah had all the luck!

'You're supposed to be in Marrakesh,' she called calmly. 'Not searching for Humphrey Bogart.'

'The house is ten minutes by bus from the centre of Marrakesh city,' answered Hannah gleefully, sizzling with excitement.

'Oh, yes? In that case, it'll have wall-to-wall cockroaches, no running water and smelly drains.'

Blue eyes crinkling, Hannah laughed.

'No problem. I'll get the haughty Khalil on his knees catching bugs, and stuffing rods down the drains to unblock them. Anyway, there must be water about, or there wouldn't be an orange grove, would there? And I've got lemon trees and date palms, and a courtyard...'

Frankie finally gained solid ground and turned to her excitedly gesticulating friend. Frankie's face softened as always at Hannah's incredibly exuberant beauty. The Moroccan men wouldn't know what had hit them, she thought.

And as for Khalil ben Hrima, he'd regret he'd once insulted and humiliated Hannah. Because now she was even lovelier than she had been. She'd shed the rather cold sophistication she'd affected then, and become more like her true self, full of vivacity and oozing self-confidence.

With that magnificent hair and her terrific figure, she'd be irresistible. A chill ran through Frankie. Did Hannah really mean it when she said the granite-hearted Khalil could never hurt her now?

'...and I'll be sunbathing...'

Hannah was still chattering on, her hands still waving about as if they had a life of their own.

'This is meant to be a working trip,' chided Frankie, interrupting. 'You won't have time for that. Anyway, it's January. It'll be raining.'

'You're green with envy!' Hannah grinned. 'Marrakesh will be gloriously warm.'

'Did you order your money?' asked the practical Frankie.

'No. I couldn't. You can't get Moroccan money over here. I'll have to change it when I arrive,' said Hannah. 'I did get my injections done, though.' She frowned and rubbed her left arm ruefully. 'The doctor grumbled because I shouldn't have left it so late. He reckons I'll have a reaction. I told him I hadn't had a *minute* free till now.'

She smiled at her friend and then hugged her. 'Isn't all this exciting? I'm far too elated to feel ill. Now…how can I casually tell everyone on the plane tomorrow where I live? It's quite a conversation stopper, isn't it, to say you rent a house with Pick-Your-Own fruit on the road to Casablanca. It sounds *wonderfully* romantic.'

'Romantic?' said Frankie incredulously. 'Is this my extrovert, thick-skinned friend talking? I'd say you were enthusiastic, cheerful, optimistic and had a tendency to speak in capital letters, but never did I imagine you could go dreamy on me.'

Hannah leapt out of the way of a workman carrying a plank, giving him a slashing grin which unsteadied him for a moment. Frankie sighed. No one did much work when Hannah was around. It was like compulsively watching a dragonfly—or a beautiful butterfly—knowing it would be elsewhere in two minutes and making the most of its colourful display while you could.

'Khalil once said,' mused Hannah, 'that I wouldn't recognise romance even if I was force-fed a thousand roses sandwiched between a shopful of Valentine's cards.'

'Nasty. Morocco's self-appointed Ego-Crusher. It'll be like the Clash of the Titans when you meet him tomorrow. Sure you want to use him as our contact?'

Hannah confidently tossed back her hair, vigorously pushing it behind her ears, as if preparing to do battle now.

'Who else do we know out there? And who else do we know who speaks seventy-nine languages faultlessly and who could have taught Machiavelli a thing or two if they'd both lived in the same century? We need a sharp cookie: someone who can out-barter the wiliest salesmen in the world. He owes me a few favours, I reckon,' she said darkly.

'Overlooking your exaggerations, I'd say he owes you your heart,' said Frankie drily. 'He took it away and I think he still owns it.'

'Don't be ridiculous!' Hannah looked genuinely astonished. 'He does nothing for me. Look!' she held out her steady hands and kept them still for a moment. 'Not a tremor! The world doesn't come skidding to a halt when I speak his name. I couldn't even contemplate working with him otherwise. Besides, I'm almost family.'

Frankie gave her an old-fashioned look. 'Oh, yes. But you both blew it. You dreamed of being his wife, once.'

Hannah winced slightly at the word. 'I meant,' she said with a shade of sharpness in her tone, 'that his step-father and I were like father and daughter. Khalil and I shouldn't remain enemies. Time we buried the hatchet. That's what he suggested, in his letter agreeing to act for us.'

'And then demanded a hefty commission,' said Frankie cynically.

'The man is necessary to us,' said Hannah firmly. 'So we'll use him. I don't hold grudges, you know that. I can't be doing with harking back to the past—the present is enough for me to handle. The man's after a fast buck. OK, I'll make him earn it. But you can't deny, he's essential to our success. Without him, we fail. We'd have no chance of judging the quality of what we're getting, or the right price to pay; the Board of Trade made that clear. A Marrakesh *souk* isn't the place for greenhorns. I doubt he gives a damn about me; probably doesn't even remember he said I was an immoral little bitch,' she said cheerfully.

'He might be hoping to get his hands on your body again,' said Frankie, looking worried. 'You know what men think about bubbly blondes with figures like yours. And he's an Arab.'

'Half-Berber,' corrected Hannah. 'As proud as hell and paranoic about his honour. Khalil? Touch me?' She shook her head emphatically. 'He's a prude and he disapproves of me. It would be like plunging his hand into donkey droppings.'

Frankie was convulsed with laughter and Hannah grinned at the thought of the immaculate, superior Khalil soiling his carefully manicured fingers.

She smiled at her friend. 'Khalil ben Hrima has got a great head for business,' she said happily. 'He wants to be cut in on our idea because he realises that our plan is an absolute *wow*!'

Hannah looked around the building, empty but for the workmen, with shining eyes. The two women linked arms and stared up at the blueprints, tacked to a makeshift notice-board on the wall. Frankie, an old schoolfriend, had inherited money from a devoted, rich uncle, and had largely financed the development. For her part, Hannah was the buyer, the persuader, and 'front of house'. Both of them had realised that she was the one who had the ability to make things hum, to make things happen.

Grateful for her friend's financial faith, Hannah was determined to overcome any obstacles, even her dislike of her ex-boss's stepson, in order to bring their plans to fruition.

It was an ambitious plan. But simple. Soon this huge warehouse would be transformed into a bustling, exotic Moroccan *souk*, with a central walkway covered in bamboo and palm leaves, and with colourful stalls on either side selling goods of every description.

She was about to embark on a buying spree in Marrakesh, purchasing traditional carpets, fabric, *djellabas* and kaftans, pottery, copper and brass, silver,

spices . . . whatever she could find to fill each little booth
with a taste of Morocco, where Africa, Arabia and
Europe met in a brilliant confusion of colour and style.
And she'd chosen Marrakesh as her starting point because she'd read so much about it already. Plus the bonus
that Khalil himself knew the city better than any man.

Her fingers idly traced the proposed outline of the
restaurant, which would be run by Frankie's brother.
There would be a tiny café, too, selling mint tea and
coffee, with plenty of sweet pastries. Maybe they'd rent
booths to working craftsmen, to draw tourists. There
were so many possibilities!

The prospect had put new life into her after Dermot's
death, and the next two miserable years working in an
insurance company, fending off the men there who
seemed to think that any single woman was fair game.
Now excitement spilled from her in a visible stream of
energy, every movement and every decision she made
being strong and positive. At twenty-four, she was finally her own woman: powerful, sure where she was
heading, exhilarated, unstoppable.

No longer did she play down her assets. Her hair was
thick and wavy and she let it hang in a heavy mass as a
bold, bright statement of her confidence. No longer did
she hide her figure to protect herself from men's avid
stares. This was her body—why should she be ashamed
of it? Why flatten her breasts just because some men
might get the wrong idea?

She smiled, wondering how her flamboyance would
go down in the *souks* of Marrakesh. This one, here in
London, had been entirely her own idea. She'd nour-
ished it secretly ever since Dermot had talked to her about
Marrakesh, his beloved city, and when she had read his
atmospheric novels.

She'd worked for the famous Irish author when she'd
left her London secretarial school shortly before her

eighteenth birthday, and had been entranced with his descriptions of Moroccan life. He'd been dying even then, and they had returned to his home in Ireland. Without parents of her own, and brought up briskly in a children's home, she'd felt rudderless till Dermot had become her protector, and she had protected him, too, in her own way.

They'd loved each other. He was her first experience of love. But *not* as a man and woman. That had been Khalil's accusation. Away from the public gaze—where Dermot O'Neill maintained a witty, wild and wicked image—they'd lived in a quiet, gentle way.

His affection had been plain for all to see. Maybe that had been the trouble. Hannah sighed and ran her fingers through her hair. Dermot had once told her that he'd never known a woman with yards of corrugated yellow wool on her head before—a slur on her glossy golden waves, but one she'd taken with a pinch of salt. For she'd noticed that women had appeared in his stories who looked like her: lively, full of optimism, never letting the harsh world get her down. It had been his lesson to her—one she'd taken to heart: 'Don't let the world lay you out on the canvas. Keep punching. Stay upright till the last round.'

He'd done just that, himself, and it had taken four years of pain before the hell-raising Dermot had allowed death to overtake him at the age of fifty-one. She was shattered by the loss. And afterwards, his vitriolic, disapproving stepson Khalil had viciously put the knife into her, venting his resentment of her attachment to Dermot by releasing a string of cruel lies to the gutter Press...

'I'll miss you,' said Frankie suddenly.

Hannah fought back the momentary sadness of her thoughts. She'd miss Frankie, too. Two months was a long time in a foreign land she'd never seen.

'Mmm. I'll miss one or two things, as well. Like...oh, the rain, the cold east wind, the constant greyness, the...' Hannah ducked as her friend waved her small fist threateningly. 'Pity me! Think how awful it'll be!' she teased. 'All the relentless sunshine and the boredom of sitting in my own little courtyard for lunch, tossing date stones at marauding donkeys——'

Frankie groaned. 'If I were better-looking, vastly experienced in the ways of men like you and not so ridiculously innocent, I'd slug you right now, grab your ticket and whoop it up in Marrakesh in your place. As it is, you'll have a ball. The Casablanca Road will be lined with parked donkeys, and their owners will be camping under your wretched orange trees with their tongues hanging out.'

Hannah's smile faded. Even her friend believed all the stories she'd read. Innocence wasn't something easily associated with Hannah Jordan. She'd been labelled as Dermot O'Neill's mistress for years and the taunts had long since ceased to wound her.

'Well, if I see any men with lolling tongues, I'll push a lemon in their mouths,' she said wryly. 'Dalliance is out. I won't have the time. Nor do I intend to handle my purchasing by doing a belly-dance and offering to spend a few hours in someone's harem. This body,' she said, dramatically placing a hand on her breast, and making the nearby tiler drop his trowel as his eyes lingered helplessly on her generous curves and his imagination ran riot. 'This body,' she repeated, oblivious to the confusion she was causing, 'won't be the price for any commercial bargains.'

Frankie dragged her eyes from the red-faced tiler.

'Oh. Shame. Think of the savings we'd make! Won't you even consider bestowing a few kisses in the direction of one or two warehouse owners? We could get everything at rock-bottom price if you did...'

'If I thought you were serious for one moment,' laughed Hannah, 'I'd ask Dave over there to build a slave market in the foyer, and get you swiftly bought up and transported to Timbuktu. Besides, you can be sure that the dreaded Khalil will set the police on me if I put a foot wrong, let alone allow my mouth to go astray. He'll be watching me like a hawk, in case I corrupt someone.'

'Typical hypocritical male. Him and his double standards! I hope you give him hell. He sounds an absolute prig,' said Frankie sympathetically.

'He's a real Miss Prim,' Hannah replied fervently. 'But he won't get a chance to question my morals. I can handle him now.'

She was too tough to permit an old, brief, flame to stir her senses. As she walked thoughtfully to her flat on the top floor of the warehouse building, she mused that it had been Dermot who'd given her the strength to shrug off the slurs on her character and to fight pain and sorrow. Khalil's betrayal of her had put that strength to the test, and she had come out of the episode stronger and harder than ever before, her emotions protected under lock and key. Gradually the realities of life had changed her character irrevocably, and sometimes Hannah longed for the naïve, eager girl she once had been.

But then she wouldn't be setting off on the most exciting adventure of her life! Nor would she feel able to travel to a Muslim country alone and set up business deals—with Khalil employed to make sure she wasn't ripped off. She frowned. Maybe that would be his revenge: to make her pay more than she ought to, and then lounge back and laugh up his sleeve at his cleverness. He wasn't to be underestimated. She'd have to go very carefully with him. Like her, he'd come a long way in a short time and was probably pretty calculating now.

He hadn't been like that when they'd first met six years ago, in Dermot's house in Ireland. She'd only been with Dermot a month and was very impressionable. Khalil would have impressed any woman.

Unable to prevent herself, she became reflective, remembering with a pang that meeting with the gentle, extraordinarily handsome man of twenty-four, who had knocked her sideways with his courtesy, his unassuming charm and his unobtrusive strength of mind.

She was so used to being flirted with and admired that the usual approaches from men meant nothing to her; they were a normal part of life. With Khalil, she felt as if she'd been hit between the eyes. All her composure vanished; she fell for him almost instantly and he swiftly became the centre of her life. From the first, it was as if he'd been tailor-made for her. If they were separated during the day, she continually looked for him, finding herself incomplete. When he joined her, they both gazed at one another in helpless, loving delight, unable to believe their luck.

He had treated her like Dresden china, as if afraid of frightening her with his passion; even more afraid of hers, because she saw no reason to hold back from the man she loved. Yet, after three weeks, he'd left without saying goodbye. Hannah was totally bewildered. Gently, Dermot told her that there was a family crisis in Marrakesh. She waited.

But Khalil never contacted her, or answered her hesitant letters, until that terrible evening when Dermot died. And by then he'd changed, no longer her tender lover, but a hard and insensitive cynic.

Sad, fleeting love. A sharp sourness hit the pit of her stomach. She bit her lip. It was past. It was over. Feeling a sense of shame and humiliation wouldn't help now.

Sobered by her memories, Hannah forced herself to pack and get ready for her trip. Usually, sharing the flat with Frankie worked well. This time, perhaps because Hannah was conscious that her arm was swelling up, she felt quite irritable. She wanted to feel on top form when she met Khalil. And to look *fantastic*.

'You don't normally spend so long putting endless coats of varnish on your nails,' said her friend. 'And why have you tried on six outfits to wear on the plane? Surely all this isn't in aid of the man you're meeting?'

'He's not a man. He's a nasty, evil shark,' muttered Hannah crossly, wishing she had time to go to the hairdresser.

'Are you sure you're over him?' asked Frankie astutely.

'Of course! I was a starry-eyed teenager——'

'You mooned over him for years,' said Frankie. 'You mustn't forget that, as your friend, I have insider knowledge.'

'My early letters to you from Ireland were full of exaggerations, as usual,' snapped Hannah. 'Besides, I know what his real nature is now. Beneath the charm lurks a cross between a cobra and a plague-carrying rat.'

'Oh, dear, he did dig deep, didn't he?' murmured Frankie.

'Don't worry, I filled in the hole again. I learnt my lesson. Giving yourself leaves you unprotected. Now—well, I defy any man to find my heart. It was swept away with the stars and moon and all the other junk,' said Hannah, a grim line to her full mouth.

But, the next day, something within her stirred when she finally caught sight of Marrakesh from the little window in the plane, late in the afternoon. The cloud which had hidden the view suddenly lifted, and, like drawing aside seven veils at once, a scene of breathtaking beauty was revealed.

Below them was a fertile plain of rich red soil, scattered with trees and fields of young barley shoots in an improbable emerald-green. Behind the low flat-roofed buildings, which were the same red as the soil, soared incredibly tall palm trees. They managed somehow to look like elongated exclamation marks, exploding at the very top with a coronet of arching fronds.

And, when the plane banked, every passenger on board gasped at the sight of Marrakesh's castellated walls enclosing a rose-pink city with its distant and magnificent backdrop: a mighty wall of white, jagged mountains. The High Atlas.

Hannah found she was holding her breath as she stared in wonder at the fabled snowy mountains, which seemed so near—forty miles away, if she remembered correctly. Dermot had said you could reach them in a couple of hours from Marrakesh. Could she see them from her little house, too? Another hour, and she'd know! Sooner than that, she'd be meeting Khalil...

Her head felt strangely heavy, probably from the dryness of the air-conditioning in the plane. Determined not to give her old enemy a chance to see any weakness anywhere, she mustered all her poise and swept through the arrivals lounge, drawing envious glances and a few covetous ones from the holidaymakers who'd flown on the same plane.

'Mademoiselle 'anna Jourdain?'

This was it. She composed herself anew, checked the elegant crushed linen suit in the same grass-green as her emerald ring from Dermot, and beckoned to the man in a fez and long white robes holding up a placard with her name on it.

'Here!' she called. Then she remembered that French was the second language here, from the long period of colonisation. Pity—her only French came from old movies. *'Ici,'* she tried hopefully.

The man grinned widely, admiring her without offence, and let out a stream of French, all of which was unintelligible. But, from his manner, it was obvious that she was to accompany him. Her heart hammering stupidly, she tipped up her head and strode along behind him, her steel-tipped high heels sounding rather bossy. They had been a deliberate choice.

Power dressing, that was what she'd opted for. She knew very well how Khalil could crush her with a look, a telling phrase. This time, she was armour-plated. It was only a business meeting, anyway, and Khalil was virtually working for her. An employee. Not a man who'd once touched his lips to hers in an angry, desperate kiss so hot, so violent, that...

She saw him. And her heart lurched, stopped, faltered, and for a moment the raw pain in her eyes was so naked that she had to pretend that she was searching in her handbag for some documents. Once again, incredibly, she could feel his searching mouth and the confusing dual sensations of hunger and satisfaction that his kisses had aroused.

She stifled a groan. Oh, curse him! He *would* be standing in profile to her! How could he be more good-looking, more darkly compelling, than she'd ever remembered? Why had time strengthened his bearded jaw, widened his shoulders, and artfully dressed him in a black suit which needed no padding on that powerful body?

I am gorgeous, his attitude seemed to be saying. Look at me and wonder.

Hannah thinned her mouth, seeing the stares from the passengers. Everyone else might be impressed, but she darn well wasn't. She counted her breath in and out, twenty times. Her eyes strayed to him again. Devastating. His starched white shirt set off his gorgeous tanned face and neck, and painfully she recalled how smooth his skin felt to the touch.

Infuriated by the effect of a man's mere skin and bone, and the way his features were arranged, Hannah grappled with her passport and gripped it tightly so that no one could see how much her hands trembled. She almost groaned. Her fingertips themselves actually remembered the satin of his skin. They were relentlessly sending back messages to her brain, making it whirl with erotic sensation.

What an imbecile she was! She couldn't revert to being eighteen just because her body had fanciful memories! Granted, he was wickedly handsome, but she didn't have to turn somersaults in full view of everyone because of that. Handsome is as handsome does, as her house parents in the children's home used to say.

Her stomach swooped. He was turning in her direction. And instantly the chilling look on his face quelled her churning emotions, slowing their heat and making them run ice-cold like a glacier. His eyes—those bottomless brown wells she'd once been submerged in— were as hard and as glittering as the frosted snow on the lofty mountains. His whole demeanour showed his utter disapproval of her. She froze. Poles apart they certainly were! The Arctic seemed to be meeting the Antarctic. There was one devil of a frost building up in between. Morocco's climate had taken a nose-dive.

Khalil's upper lip curved in disdain as his wintry gaze slowly descended over her brightly tumbling mass of hair, her carefully thickened mascara-black eyelashes, and the full red lips, now pouting a little in resentment.

With cynicism clear in his eyes, he took in the arrogant set of her shoulders, squared in defence and emphasising the aggressive shoulder-pads. Distaste shaped the carved lines of his mouth as his eyes lingered where her breasts jutted firmly beneath the vivid green jacket.

That didn't stop him from touring the whole of their outline, though. She withstood the long-drawn-out onslaught, her anger rising as the extent of his contempt became more and more obvious. Who the hell did he think he was? Defender of the Faith? Protector of his countrymen?

A small lift of Khalil's deep chest accompanied his scrutiny of her small waist and curving hips, then, after a cursory sweep of his lashes in the direction of her long slender legs, he flicked his gaze upwards and their eyes clashed.

Blue blaze met brown. He lifted one haughty eyebrow. Hannah was quivering with bottled-up rage and he could see that. It seemed to please him.

'I could light a fire with the sparks from your eyes,' he murmured huskily.

Taken unawares by the forgotten richness of his voice, she fought for sanity, furiously struggling to bring her wayward senses under control. For they were still in the past, when his voice had had the power to drive hotly into her soul and fill her head with foolishness. She should have remembered. She should have been prepared.

'I? Light fires? Not inside you, I hope,' she retorted tartly, fear making her go into the attack. 'I'd hate to melt the frozen ice beneath that Marks and Spencer suit and bring a dinosaur back to life.'

'No danger,' he grated, ignoring the jibe about his expensive tailoring. 'I've never been excited by the offer of cheap goods.'

She gave a quick intake of breath. 'Do you mean me?' she asked in amazement.

He shrugged his broad shoulders elegantly. 'If the label fits, Hannah...'

As if he couldn't care less about her, he turned to the man with the placard. *'Merci, mon ami,'* he said, handing him some coins, then flicking her a mocking, superior glance. 'Welcome to Marrakesh, Hannah.'

It was the least sincere remark she'd ever heard. She had been digesting the fact that open war still existed between them. So be it, she thought. I've never pulled my punches. He'll get as good as he gives. However compelling, however charismatic he is, Khalil will discover that I can be as tough as he.

She clasped her hands together and put on an awed expression. 'Gee, gosh, thanks! Who could fail to be knocked sideways by your welcome? Anyone who lived in a snake-pit would feel instantly at home. Your grudging hospitality and shy, awkward charm overwhelm me, as usual.'

'Well, you haven't changed,' he said, a glacial light in his eyes. 'Still the same sarcastic bitch.'

'Who else but a bitch would know how to deal with a dog?' she retorted coolly. 'Shall we find my luggage and get me to the place I'm renting before I embarrass us both?'

'Embarrass?' He frowned, going on ahead and sending a puzzled look over his shoulder in her direction. 'In what way?'

She smiled brilliantly all through the perfunctory Customs check, and let her lashes flutter deceptively at Khalil. Arrogant men were easily managed by the simple means of disconcerting them.

'It's wicked of me, I know, but I always have an uncontrollable urge to embarrass pompous men in public. My usual method is to fling myself at their feet and weep.' She assessed the cleanliness of the floor and batted her eyes at him innocently. 'I thought I might scream hysterically and pretend you've deserted me and our nineteen children, or——'

'That's not funny, Hannah! I've seen enough of your dangerous play-acting in the past. Don't begin your flippant and stupid conversations with me around,' he said harshly, a ferocious glare drawing his black brows together.

Her air of innocence departed and she fixed him with a chilling blast of her ice-blue eyes.

'Then don't push me,' she retorted through clenched teeth. 'You don't own the copyright on insults or bad manners. Why should I put up with your taunts? Treat me like a normal human being and I won't be tempted to shock you or act outrageously. Try my temper, and I'll behave as if I really *am* the kind of woman you imagine me to be.'

Unconsciously, she'd struck a defiant pose, her head high, her hair blazing in a gold halo behind her as if that too was on fire. Khalil hissed in his breath and his cheekbones stood out high where his face had suddenly hollowed. He abruptly turned on his heel, his back to her.

Hannah was incensed by his bad manners. She actually had to walk around him, to confront him boldly, the light of battle in her eyes. She hadn't finished with him yet. If he thought he'd crush her with a few well-chosen words, he was mistaken.

'Shall we get something clear before we go any further?' she suggested in tones of loathing. 'I've come here with every intention of forgetting the past and starting afresh. There's no need for personal feelings to come into our business deal. You agreed to act as my contact here, at a commission on our profits which is very favourable to you, and I think you should put aside everything else and honour that agreement. Don't you?'

He smiled. And it was a slow, sensual smile which drove deep into her, awakening chords which he'd once brought so disastrously to life.

'I do. I hadn't meant to insult you.' He gave a slight laugh of self-mockery. 'Not openly, anyway,' he admitted with shattering honesty. 'Unfortunately, I'd forgotten how...' His eyes wandered insolently over her and Hannah willed herself to remain calm when they met hers again, boring into her relentlessly. 'I'd forgotten what a shocking and naked sexuality you effortlessly display,' he finished, with even more candour. 'A sexuality which is even more obvious now than ever before. You're like a neon advertising sign, Hannah.'

'Only in your distorted eyesight,' she countered, nervous of his awakening sexual arousal. 'Someone once said that we tend to see things not as they are, but as *we* are. You only see what you're looking for. I don't project sexuality—I certainly wouldn't let a scrap of it come to the surface with you around. It's all in your mind.'

He grinned lazily and her knees weakened at the melting desire in his eyes. Her face flushed hot and she wondered if she was beginning to react to the injection. That was all she needed!

'No, it's not in my mind,' he said in a voice of soft silk. He pushed his hands into his trouser pockets and Hannah's eyes drifted unwillingly to the taut muscles of his thighs. 'Lust doesn't affect my *brain*. As a woman of the world, who better than you would know all about physical reactions and where they're sited?'

'You're being offensive, Khalil,' she said coldly, hating his clever manipulation of her. If he ever knew she was affected...'I think I'll make my own way to my house.'

Scornfully, she swept past him, collected her case and struggled outside with it. Immediately a group of six taxi drivers descended on her, chattering in French and broken English, bombarding her with offers—not all of which, she gathered, were purely for transportation to her destination. Men's eyes told you a lot, even if their mouths didn't, she thought wryly.

'Not today, thanks,' she said scathingly to one, who spoke quite good English. 'I don't want you to take me to bed. How about taking me to this address, instead?'

'You *are* confident.' The address was slipped neatly from her hand. 'So that's where you're living. I have my car,' continued Khalil smoothly. 'It would be a shame not to use it, wouldn't it? I imagine you don't have any Moroccan money yet.'

'No, but I can change some here,' she said haughtily.

He smiled. 'Sadly, the desk at the airport is closed. Now where does that leave you? I fear,' he said huskily, moistening his lips, 'that you might be forced to sell something to pay for the trip.'

His expression left her in no doubt as to what he thought she might be willing to sell. Hannah's temper rose so fast at the deliberate insult that she had slapped Khalil's face before she knew what she was doing. The shock electrified them both.

CHAPTER TWO

THEY stood glaring at each other, and the taxi drivers melted away. She was horrified at her action, but incapable of apologising. He'd deserved that. Her fingers tingled from the contact with him. Smooth skin, soft beard. Warm. The fragrance he favoured had drifted over her nostrils, tantalising her with memories. Her lips parted.

The mark of her hand still on his cheek, Khalil's chest expanded to its full extent and she saw a glittering menace in his eyes before his lids dropped to hide their expression.

'I'm not apologising,' she snapped.

To her relief he had mastered his rage, and when he lifted his lashes again she saw nothing but mockery.

'Physical contact can be so exciting, can't it?' he murmured. 'And anger. We do arouse each other, don't we, Hannah?'

'I think,' said Hannah, incensed, 'that you've got the wrong idea about me.'

'No,' he said softly. 'I don't think so.'

She looked at him in angry despair. If they couldn't work together without him trying to seduce her, then she really would have to manage alone.

'Khalil, we made a mistake. This isn't going to work,' she said briskly. 'But, since you're here, I might as well make use of you. You can give me a lift, since I only have English money on me. After that, we'll say goodbye. I'll manage my business without you,' she said, meeting him squarely in the eyes.

24

'No, you won't,' he responded smugly. 'You need me, Hannah.'

'As I need poison,' she snapped, irritated by his arrogance.

He raised a dark eyebrow.

'I don't think you realise the difficulties of buying goods in my country. For a start, you're a woman——'

'Meaning that male dominance is the norm, and that women are only for sex and babies?' she asked sarcastically.

'No.' He frowned. 'Women here have equal constitutional rights with men. They can be lawyers, doctors, whatever. Don't bring your prejudices here. This is a tolerant country.'

'Prejudices? I was only basing my knowledge of Marrakesh on your chauvinistic attitude to me,' she said sweetly.

'And Dermot's out of date and highly imaginative books,' he commented grimly. 'Nevertheless, I can't deny that in the *souks* you'd find it difficult as a foreign buyer. You're not shopping in Oxford Street. You've entered a very different world from the one you know. I see you still speak no French, and doing business will be impossible.'

She went cold, suddenly seeing the whole of her future crumbling away. Did he hate her that much? Was this his revenge? A passage in one of Dermot's books came into her mind to haunt her.

> The people of the High Atlas exist in snow and heat and know no grey in their lives, only black and white, the twin passions of love and hate. Beware their love. It will consume you. Beware their hatred. It will freeze blood.

Hers was freezing already. Her confidence and euphoria began to drain away. Khalil must hate her very, very much. Her own sense of misguided pride had allowed him to think that she was his stepfather's mistress, even while she and Khalil had been lovers.

Suddenly Hannah yearned for the truth to be known. She was sick of turning a blind eye to the way people regarded her; tired of shrugging off their nasty-minded and misguided assessments of her character. Inexplicably, despite Dermot's insistence that you never lowered yourself to explain, that you never defended any scurrilous Press reports, she could think of nothing else but her overwhelming desire to prove her integrity to Khalil. It was very important—he'd treat her better, he'd see her as a business colleague instead of an immoral, scheming whore. She must somehow convince him that it was possible to be outgoing, outspoken and confident, yet still have scruples and live a moral life.

A small and rueful smile of realisation touched her lips. He'd never believe anything she said! There was only one way she could really show him that she'd never been any man's mistress, let alone his stepfather's: physical proof! It was a price she wasn't prepared to pay, even to clear her good name.

Khalil would never believe she was a virgin, however much she protested her innocence. And, since she'd never give him the chance to find out for sure, he'd probably think badly of her forever.

Her palms felt hot and sticky. Absently she rubbed them together, thinking hard and deciding to confront him with her fears.

'Have you done this on purpose?' she asked quietly. 'Are you trying to make Frankie and me lose a great deal of money? Did you bring me out here under false pretences, after promising Frankie that there would be no difficulties——'

'Ah, yes. Frankie.' His mocking eyes considered her thoughtfully. 'That's the one who put up the money, yes?'

'You know darn well.'

Hannah hadn't felt so worried in a long time. She wouldn't put it past Khalil to have set her up. His courteous, businesslike letters had convinced her that he was interested in her development. But maybe all he wanted was her downfall.

'A...close friend?' he asked silkily.

'Frankie?' Hannah was just about to tell him that Frankie was a woman, when her sense of caution stopped her. If he thought her friend was male, then he might not try to harass her. Khalil was sufficiently Arab to think that two women in business would be a pushover if he wanted to destroy them. So she gave a secret, dreamy smile and was pleased to see Khalil's face darken. 'Frankie and I are like *that*,' she said, linking her two fingers closely together.

'You finally made it, then,' he said softly. 'You found someone rich to pay the bills.'

'I'm not what you think——' she began.

'This way,' he murmured, walking off with her suitcase.

She scowled at his retreating back and gave an infuriated sigh. Back home—even ten minutes ago—everything had seemed so well planned and she'd been looking forward to her time here. Now Khalil had spoiled it all with his acid tongue and vitriolic accusations. It was a habit of his. She'd been over-hopeful, thinking he'd forgotten the past.

He looked back at her, his face expressionless. Pursing her lips she gave him a baleful stare and proudly followed, taking her time, sauntering slowly with a swing to her shoulders. She refused to lose command of the situation.

He stood watching her progress cynically, as she ran the gauntlet of drivers and guides, tourists and businessmen, all of whom paused to admire her queenly advance.

Khalil held open the door of a large new Mercedes, and took her elbow to help her in.

'I'm perfectly capable of getting into a car on my own,' she snapped.

'It was a courtesy,' he said, a hasty smile stretching his briefly tightened lips. 'Habit.' He watched her endless legs swing into the car. 'Don't you like me to behave like a gentleman?'

She waited till he'd settled in the driving seat.

'Why be a hypocrite?' she asked coolly. 'We both know you're not a gentleman in any shape or form.'

He grinned at her. 'Wait till you get in the old town. You'll find out what real harassment is like.' His eyes assessed her body critically and Hannah tried to stare him down. 'I hope you've got a wig and some restricting corsets.'

'What do you mean?' she frowned.

He switched on the ignition and drove out of the airport.

'I'm afraid the behaviour of some western women leaves much to be desired. Many of them are very…eager for sex,' he drawled, his mouth unnervingly sensual as he contemplated the idea. 'And you'll find that prostitutes work undercover—if you'll pardon the pun—because they're banned. They're identifiable by the fact that they tend to be bold, brassy and blonde and move around alone. Like you. It would be difficult for an innocent Marrakshi man to tell the difference. I can guarantee that, within minutes of entering the markets, you'll be surrounded, jostled, touched, brushed up against, propositioned...'

'Not if I have a guide,' she protested, privately aghast.

'What the hell do you think the guide's going to be doing all this time?' he murmured lazily. 'He'll be trying to get you into a dark alley, too. You mustn't blame the men. They'd be responding to your apparently open invitation. Sex breathes from every one of your pores, Hannah.'

'I don't believe what you're saying——'

'No? Try it and see.'

She sat in silence. She had read reports, of course, in the guidebooks, that the custom was for Moroccan women to be circumspect in the way they looked, and that European women could be mistakenly seen as provocative and their friendliness misinterpreted. But...oh, curse Khalil for being so difficult to get on with! He would have been an ideal deterrent! He had the ability to wither every bloom in the Chelsea Flower Show with one look!

Within the car, the blistering hostility seared between them in a crackling undercurrent. It charged the atmosphere with a dangerous electricity and built up to such a pitch that Hannah felt she'd burst if she didn't say anything.

She wanted to enjoy her arrival. This was one of the great Imperial Cities of Africa. Her whole introduction to Marrakesh was turning sour in her mouth. She couldn't stand it.

'All right,' she said grimly. 'Let's settle this. Are you trying to put obstacles in my way?'

For several seconds he concentrated on the road. Hannah stared at his implacable profile resentfully.

'No,' he said finally. 'I was. Not any more.'

'*What?*' she gasped in disbelief.

She noticed that every one of his tightly tensed muscles was relaxing, one by one. Her eyes were drawn to them, fascinated: the high carriage of his shoulders dropping, his chest deflating in a long exhalation of breath, the material stretched over his swollen thighs softening into folds and the hard, muscular legs shifting to an easier position. And then he flashed her a charming, apologetic smile.

'I admit it,' he said disarmingly. 'I wanted to take my revenge for the way you used me. When you contacted me, it seemed as if you'd played into my hands. My quick-tempered Berber blood began to take over my senses. Do you remember, Hannah, that I told you I was a savage child of the mountains?'

He'd said very little about his background when they'd been in love. Only that he was a Marrakshi guide, and that his mother was a Berber woman.

Most of their brief and passionate romance had been spent in enjoying the Irish countryside and exchanging sweet and increasingly desperate kisses. She hadn't wanted to know too much about him. That would have meant confronting the differences in their cultures, and she had been afraid to spoil their happiness with problems.

'I can't say I do recall much,' she said crushingly, rejecting her painful memories by appearing to examine the passing scenery. She didn't see a thing. Only a couple on an Irish hillside, embracing avidly amid the buttercups.

'Really. Well, take a tip from our king. He's wise enough to know that the Berbers are not submissive by nature, nor are we orthodox.'

'Once you were polite,' said Hannah, a lump in her throat, briefly swept back to that vulnerable innocence of her youth. He'd been so gentle. She would have trusted him with her soul. Darn it, she *had* trusted him with her soul!

'I still am,' he said quietly. 'You just got under my skin for a short time. That made me even more annoyed. I don't often have the bad manners to confront someone and let them know that they've offended me.'

'What do you mean?' She frowned.

'We are not directly insulting to our enemies, let alone our friends. Friendship in particular is sacred to me—to all Moroccans. Everyone is a potential friend. We believe that it is the height of rudeness to jeopardise a friendship,' he murmured. 'So if a friend—or even an acquaintance—hurts one of us, or says something he disagrees with, he keeps his own counsel.'

'That's hypocritical——'

'No. It's putting one value higher than another. Friendship comes before our own needs. We're willing to swallow our pride rather than lose a friend by trying to push our point of view—which could be misguided, anyway.'

'At least you admit you're not infallible! And what about those enemies?' she asked cynically. 'No wonder you're devious! You stab them in the back?'

His mouth twisted as he smiled to himself.

'An enemy is a friend you have lost.' Khalil let out a slow breath. 'You were once a friend, Hannah.' His jaw tightened. 'More than that,' he added, his voice soft in his throat.

She dragged her eyes away from his murmuring lips, feeling her whole self become tender and pliable. Those memories of hers had made her soft! He was trying to charm her, to start it all up again, for his own self-satisfaction. And then he'd toss her away like a piece of discarded wrapping, just as he had before. But she refused to be hurt again. The scars were too deep. If they were opened up again, she'd lose all her glorious strength and independence.

He shot her a glance, his long lashes lazily flickering over her stony face.

'Out of all the women I've ever known——'

'Save your flowery words, Khalil,' she said coldly. 'You're polluting the atmosphere with your lies. Can't you see I don't give a fig about you?'

'I know that. You don't let emotions get in the way of your practical needs. That makes you even more appealing to me. A woman who takes what she wants, whatever it is. How can I help but notice your earthiness? Every time I look at you, I see...' His husky voice trailed away. Khalil seemed to be recalling a long-distant memory too.

'I can't bear the suspense,' she said drily. 'What do you see?'

'Sex,' he breathed, giving the word a warm and deeply sensual sound. 'I told you. Hot, raw, responding sensuality, that's what I see. So would any man with half an eye.'

'I'd black that half-eye if he tried anything,' she warned.

'What an aggressive woman you've become,' crooned Khalil, not at all crushed. 'Reacting violently because I respond to your open invitation.'

'I thought you weren't excited by cheap goods?' she reminded him haughtily.

'So did I,' he growled throatily. 'I was wrong, wasn't I?'

Hannah felt alarmed at the warning signs in his smouldering eyes. 'I see no reason to play down the way I look just because you're foolish enough to judge a book by its cover,' she said tightly.

'If a book has a lurid jacket, it gives an indication of what to expect if you pick it up,' he commented.

'Heavens! I'd hate to be picked up and thumbed by you. I'd rather discard my lurid jacket and swathe myself in a kaftan and a veil,' she said, with a toss of her hair.

'A good idea, if you're intending to wander around. Your sexy appearance might be too much for the men of Marrakesh.'

He was right. She'd actually brought some inoffensive, sober clothes with her because of that fact. Dressing and behaving as she wanted to had its drawbacks even in England. No boyfriend had ever seen past her physical attributes. Men were so single-minded and disappointing.

She wondered what to do, wanting to get back on to a businesslike footing with Khalil without losing face by apologising. She did need him, unfortunately—that was becoming painfully clear.

'I said I had wanted to make life as difficult for you as possible,' he said. 'However, I've changed my mind——'

'Why?' she asked, not trusting him.

'Because I can see that you're even tougher than before. I think you'll make a great success of this venture of yours and, as the Americans say,' he grinned, laughing at some private joke, 'I want a "piece of the action". I'll show you around Marrakesh and help you to choose your purchases wisely, pay the right price and arrange shipments, as we agreed in writing.'

Hannah passed a hand over her hot forehead to ease the throbbing there. It seemed she was starting a headache.

'And you accuse *me* of putting aside my feelings for the sake of commercial gain?' she asked scornfully, curving both hands around her burning neck and lifting up her hair to cool herself down.

'We were very close, once, Hannah,' he said in a husky whisper which made her skin prickle. 'We can never reach that innocence again. It's been lost, for both of us. But we're capable of forming another relationship. Different, but equally satisfying.'

She let her tongue slip out in a tiny movement, to moisten her dry, fevered lips, flinching when he growled deep in his throat at the gesture.

'Khalil,' she croaked, wondering what had happened to her voice. He'd think she was aroused by him. He already had a bad opinion of her morals, and that was offensive enough.

They were approaching the castellated ochre walls and travelling along a wide boulevard. The pavements on either side were lined with heavily laden orange trees, but the sight of them did nothing to lift Hannah's spirits. Her head had become heavy and she felt as if she were on fire.

'Yes,' he said softly, reaching out and touching her arm briefly. 'We'll make a good team. It'll be a very profitable venture.'

She blinked, feeling a great sense of relief. She'd been so wary of him, so much on her guard, that she'd overestimated his attraction to her. He was a mercenary devil, after all. He saw her as a means of making a lot of money. That suited her, though she'd have to make sure he wasn't getting backhanders from the men he introduced her to.

'Providing we keep it on a business level, I think we might have a deal. I'm willing to put aside my dislike of you.'

'A two-edged sword, your words of conciliation,' said Khalil drily.

They'd taken the first step. The atmosphere was less torrid, almost inhabitable. She gave a cool smile and turned her attention to the landscape, looking for something to change the conversation. On her right soared a high square tower, a striking landmark. It appeared to be a lone minaret, framed by waving green palms, backed by the wall of blue-white Atlas Mountains and rising majestically into a sky which was beginning to glow a soft sunset-pink.

'What's that?' she asked.

'The Koutoubia tower, a twelfth-century mosque,' he offered by way of explanation.

'It must be visible for miles,' she said, trying to respond politely. It was a mark of her preoccupation that she hadn't noticed it before.

'You'll find it a useful aid if you ever get lost in the city. If I remember rightly, it's two hundred and fifty feet tall. The wife of the sultan who built it broke three hours of the Ramadan fast and presented those golden balls on the top as a penance. They're guarded by genies.'

Relieved that he'd taken her cue to stick to uncontroversial subjects, Hannah laughed delightedly at the thought and wondered why his hand tightened momentarily on the wheel.

'You haven't forgotten the patter, I see. Once a guide, always a guide.'

'You remember that?' he asked, his eyes bleak.

So he loathed the memory, too, and resented the loss of his illusions about her.

Yes. She remembered everything. The hours spent with him had been run and rerun through her mind. They'd planned a visit to Marrakesh for her so that he could show her his city. That had been when they were young and in love, of course. Or rather, she had been in love.

'I remember you were a guide when we first met. And then...later, I understood from Dermot that you'd become one of the senior guides in the city; that you knew everything there was to know about Marrakesh,' she said quietly. For some reason she saw that she had annoyed him, and cast around for inspiration, seeking to keep the conversation light. 'So, tell me why there are so many policemen about? There's one on every road junction.'

'The King is in the city,' he answered curtly, accelerating past a horse and trap. 'The police carry out routine checks on every road into Marrakesh, particularly on travellers and lorries from the south, Tangier, and Casa. That's Casablanca. They also make sure he moves about easily within the city. His palace is in the centre.'

'Is it a state visit or something?'

Khalil sounded his horn loudly at a group of children, carrying huge pitchers of water on their heads and wandering carelessly into the road. Hannah was startled when he waved at them as he drove past, a sudden grin lighting his face.

'He's here for three months. He'll stay till the Feast of the Throne, in March. By then everywhere is hung with green and red flags, banners and bunting. You can see some streets have already been decorated. That's our flag, there: red with a green pentagram, the Seal of Solomon.'

Hannah nodded. 'The same shape as the Star of David,' she said. 'Odd, that, for Arabs and Jews to share the same symbol.'

'You'll find that our version of Islam here is very tolerant. We have a history of coexisting peacefully with Jews and Christians. I count many of them as my good friends. Try to grasp that, Hannah. We search for friendship, for tolerance and understanding.'

She bit back a sharp remark. He hadn't shown her any friendship or understanding. But she'd keep him talking. At least the ice was being broken a little.

'And the women? You said they could make choices. Is that why I see some dressed in yashmaks and *djellabas* and some in jeans and T-shirts? Or does that mean that some are Muslim and the others not?'

'They're all Muslim,' he answered. His eyes slanted at her. 'I don't think you'll like my answer,' he drawled.

His hand strayed to his beard for a moment, his lips parting slightly. Hannah felt her toes curl and heat wash through her again. When she got to her house, she'd take an aspirin. That would put her head straight.

'Moroccan women,' he continued, 'dress as they, and their fathers—or husbands—wish.'

'You mean, the men tell them what to wear.' She frowned.

'No. Some families, some men, some women, are liberal; others aren't. There are all sorts. Women can make a choice from the start. They have a way of not agreeing to marriage if they don't like the terms——' Khalil smiled '—and influencing their husbands after. This is an easygoing country. Women can be very choosy about their husbands.'

A sudden thought struck her, so forcibly that it sliced in a sharp pain through her chest and stunned her with its unexpected intensity. It had been so long since she'd known him. He had made a life without her.

'And you? Are...are you married?' she asked with elaborate casualness.

The knuckles of his hand grew white. She looked up and saw that his jaw had become solid. But it was the traffic which had made him tense. He was glaring at a donkey cart in front of the car. He swung around it before answering and in that space of time her heart had set up a ridiculously loud pounding. She waited for his reply with a dry mouth, furious that she should care, incapable of understanding why she didn't want any other woman to touch him, to kiss him, to know the gentle rasp of his beard on her face...

Hannah turned away and examined the scenery with a fierce intent, deliberately forcing herself to blank off her feelings by taking in every detail.

They appeared to be driving down an elegant, wide avenue, peopled by an extraordinary mixture of smartly

dressed men and women, casual tourists and Moroccan
men in their traditional hooded robes. Out there, life
ambled slowly and amiably in the warm afternoon. The
pavement cafés were packed. Everyone seemed to be
smiling and relaxed, and as laid-back as she'd imagined
from her reading. Why, then, was Khalil himself so cruel,
so harsh, so different? Hannah fidgeted uncomfortably,
her mind in turmoil, hating the stark contrast between
the peaceful scene outside and the tight, strained atmosphere which had built up again within the car.

'I'm not married.'

Khalil's voice sounded husky to her ears.

'Oh. No one good enough?' she tried to joke. But
because of her ridiculous relief, she had hardened her
voice. The phrase came out badly and made him scowl.
Hannah could have kicked herself. 'I'm sorry,' she
apologised. 'Joke. After all, I'm not married, either.'

'Oh. No one bad enough?' he murmured.

She winced, then gave a wry laugh. 'You win that
round,' she conceded.

'I didn't know we were fighting.'

'We find it hard not to.'

The flash of his white teeth disconcerted her. 'True,'
he agreed. 'I wonder why?'

Hannah struggled to remember the important point
she'd been querying. 'What I wanted to know,' she persisted, 'was if it's unusual for a man to be unmarried at
your age.'

His eyebrow lifted. 'Thirty? I admit that even in the
recent past it would have been. Men and women used
to marry very young. My mother was first married at
the age of thirteen. I'm the youngest of sixteen children.'

'Sixteen?' she gasped faintly, horrified. He'd never
said. 'That's terrible! Your poor mother——'

'A typically western response,' he mocked. 'Your
sympathy isn't needed. She was very happy. Large fam-

ilies were once encouraged, to promote the spread of Islam. Besides, having children is a delight to us, not a necessary evil consequence of sex.' He gave a chuckle at her sniff. 'You'll see very soon that we adore children here. They're called "the fruit of life".'

His face had become sweeter and Hannah dragged her eyes away from him. Men who softened at the thought of children were in danger of appealing to her deeply buried, tender heart.

'But now,' he continued, 'we marry at the same sort of ages as you do in England. So I'm not yet considered to be past it, or on the shelf,' he finished, with a smile.

'Nothing's changed here, though,' she argued. 'Your society still has a high expectation of morality. I would have thought that there was still a tradition of young marriages in order to... to...' She floundered. This was deep water!

'To control the undesirable expression of our passionate natures?' he asked, his eyes laughing at her. 'You're right, there is a problem for young and virile men. They manage to solve it, though.'

She flushed at his suggestive glance, which indicated that she might be willing to assuage some of *his* frustrations.

'I'm not interested in your sexuality,' she said in studied reproof. 'Nor in solving your particular problem. Can't you think of anything else?'

He grinned broadly. 'Not at this precise moment, no,' he murmured deep in his throat, giving her another avid glance.

Hannah heaved an over-exaggerated sigh.

'Try,' she said drily. 'Stop manoeuvring the conversation towards what appears to be your favourite subject.' She ignored his throaty chuckle and plunged on. 'Tell me, how would *you* treat your wife? What

would she wear? A *djellaba* and veil, or anything she
chose?'

He grunted. 'It would depend. If she looked like you,
I'd make her do what my mother did,' he answered
obliquely.

'Keep her busy with loads of children?' Hannah was
really curious. No one had spoken of Khalil's mother,
not even Dermot. He'd made it clear that she was taboo
in conversation.

'Well, certainly I'd want children, though that's not
what I was thinking of. I meant that a woman as blatant
a flirt as you would need to be kept behind closed doors
and never let out.'

'I don't believe you!' she cried with a derisive laugh.
'You're all talk. You're too westernised, too...'

Her voice trailed away. Khalil had lifted his head
proudly and she saw in his haughty expression all the
arrogance and severity of a fierce Berber tribesman.
Dermot again... He'd said that they dressed like beggars
and walked like kings. The pride of lions. The savagery
of tigers.

Khalil bewildered her. On the surface, his dress and
manner—and his perfect English—made him appear to
be sophisticated and European in behaviour. Yet there
was a secret, more exotic side to him, springing from a
culture she didn't understand. He was composed of so
many layers, such depth, that she'd never know the true
man inside, never discover what he really thought or
really believed in. She'd been naïve to think once that
they could have been happy together.

His behaviour towards her was contrary, and confusing. One moment she saw hatred in his eyes; the next,
there was only desire. And then he changed swiftly to
crisp efficiency, or easy courtesy. She didn't know what
to make of him at all.

'If you were my wife, Hannah, I'd lock you up,' he breathed, hypnotising her with his softly moving lips. He gave a low, mocking laugh. 'You'll never know if I mean that, will you, Hannah? We'd have to be married for you to find out.'

His hand strayed out to touch her, but she shrank against the car door, afraid he'd hurt her sore arm. And afraid he'd see her whole body quiver with his caress.

'You really ought to get your story straight. With one breath you claim there's tolerance here, with the other you pretend you'd lock up your wife,' she said harshly. 'You can hardly expect me to believe anything you say.'

'I told you. It's a matter of individual arrangement. Take my mother, for instance. As a Berber woman, she lived freely in the mountains with no restrictions. Then she married my father, a traditional city man, though they lived in her village. From that time on, even when Father died, she never set foot outside her home until her body was removed for burial.'

'Khalil! What are you saying?' cried Hannah, astounded. 'You are a liar! I know perfectly well that she married again! If she never left home, as you claim, however could she have met Dermot and become his wife? And why did they marry? Why wouldn't he talk about her——'

'It's a private, family matter,' he said tersely. 'Nothing to do with you. Mistresses don't count as family.'

'Oh! You bastard!' she cried, white with anger.

'Wrong. I was the last-born and my father died soon after my birth, but I was not a bastard. However, I understand you are,' he said calmly.

Flames of rage flooded through her and for a moment she couldn't trust herself to speak. Khalil was despicable, taunting her about her background.

'That's hardly the response of a gentleman,' she whispered.

'I'm well aware of that. You yourself said I wasn't one. You can't have it both ways. It's the response of a man who is confronted with a woman hell-bent on equality,' he answered curtly. 'If you can call me a bastard, I can do the same for you—especially if it's true.'

'I can't help my parentage,' she muttered.

'No. But you could have overcome it, instead of using your parents' lack of morals to excuse your own,' he said coldly.

'Oh, God!' she moaned, feeling limp and tired suddenly. 'Will you never listen to me? I haven't the energy to argue with you now, but before we do business together, you must hear me out, Khalil. Tomorrow. I demand that you listen to my side of that ghastly episode of two years ago.'

'I can't wait to hear what you have to say,' he growled. 'You've never bothered to explain before. Now it seems you might lose a business advantage, you're suddenly anxious to whitewash yourself.'

'It's not a whitewash!'

'No? Just remember that I wasn't brought up on fairy-stories. My childhood was spent scrabbling for dirhams from tourists, in walking for a whole day to barter with the few surplus vegetables we had, and in spending hours up on the freezing snows of the Tishka pass, trying to sell rock crystal to the occasional sightseers. I'm street-wise, Hannah. That's how I purchased land at the right price and at the right time, how I can juggle being the owner of a fashion business in Casa and restaurants in all the Imperial Cities. I've learnt to size people up and I'm never wrong.'

'You are in my case,' she said wearily.

He *had* come a long way. She'd had no idea he was so successful. The grapevine hadn't told her.

'We'll see,' he said in a voice laced with sexual menace. 'We'll see. Look. We're coming to the orchard.'

Her head lay back in defeat. He wouldn't get it into his thick skull that she was purity itself. When she felt fitter, she'd have a go at him, with all guns blazing!

Her eyes brightened a little when they turned off the main road and she peered out to see goats straggling across a rough dirt road bounded by a small olive grove. A little further on, Khalil stopped the car and lifted out Hannah's suitcase. She clambered unsteadily out to the smell of warm soil and the sound of chirruping birds. They were on a beaten earth track with a high wall which enclosed an orchard of orange and lemon trees, their lollipop-shaped canopies bright with an abundance of fruit.

She sniffed the air.

'Orange-blossom,' murmured Khalil.

'Flowers and fruit at the same time?' she asked, surprised.

'We Moroccans believe in pleasing as many of our senses at the same time as possible,' he said, the slow simmer in his eyes warming her blood.

'It's lovely,' she said brightly, not letting him spoil it for her. 'Frankie will be very jealous.'

'Oh, yes. He certainly will.'

She bit back a smile. He had been fooled, then.

Everything seemed lush and green, not what she'd expected at all. When she looked around, she could see tall date palms and green fields beyond the small farm where they stood. It seemed extraordinary that they were on the continent of Africa.

'I'm feeling hazy. I think this place must be a mirage,' she said, shutting her heavy eyes and letting the setting sun warm her drowsy lids. 'It can't be true. It's all too fertile.'

He hesitated for a moment, then plucked some blossom and pushed it into her hair, his warm fingers sensitising her ear as they secured the sprig.

For a moment, he was very close. Too close. She felt the rapid beat of her heart and despite her lowered lashes could sense every breath which came from his intensely masculine body. The rich scent of the orange-blossom threatened to swamp her senses. A heat throbbed inside her and she wondered if it *was* only her reaction to the cholera and typhoid jabs, or something infinitely more dangerous.

'More than a mirage,' he said quietly, reaching up and adjusting the blossom.

Hannah stood in frozen silence, incapable of moving. Khalil bent his head and, for one incredulous moment, she thought he meant to kiss her. His jaw slid close to hers, a tantalising hair's breadth away, his beard making her skin tighten with its butterfly touch. She felt him inhale deeply.

'Lovely,' he said, drawing back, a mocking smile on his face. 'And definitely not a mirage, is it?'

'N-n-no,' she stammered shakily.

Then glared at him. He gave her a knowing grin and she felt sure he was perfectly aware of the damnable effect he was having on her. She passed a trembling hand over her forehead and searched her muzzy brain for something banal to say.

'Fertile ground,' he said, his eyes amused.

Was he really intending a double meaning there? If so, he had a shock coming to him.

'Manure,' she said blandly.

He threw back his head and laughed, unfairly stopping Hannah's heart for one brief moment. No man should be that handsome, she thought sourly.

'The water of life,' he corrected, still with his sinful grin transforming his features.

Hannah swallowed hard. 'Is there a river near here, then? And a good system of irrigation?' she asked in a high, unnatural voice.

Khalil studied her for a second before answering, the dark pools of his eyes very serious. Hannah found it difficult to avoid them, but she had to, otherwise she'd be drowning in their treacherous depths.

'The city is a vast artificial oasis. In the eleventh century, underground channels were built to bring fresh water from the mountains, so that this should be a land of summer water. The High Atlas mountains rise to almost fourteen thousand feet,' he said quietly. 'They're covered in snow for perhaps eight months of the year. The snow-melt brings torrents of water down the valleys and on to the plains of Marrakesh. In fact, not long ago we had disastrous floods in early autumn,' he continued. 'You'll see the evidence of that if you take a trip up into the foothills.'

'I'd like that,' she said, glad that he'd lifted the pressure emanating from his insistent sensuality. 'I've read so much about them. They sound very beautiful.'

'They are. Come. I expect you want to settle in before it gets late.'

'Late? Oh, lord. You mean, there's no electric light?' asked Hannah anxiously, hurrying a little dizzily after him as he strode along what had become a tiled footpath.

'Oh, there's light. And water—a bathroom, too. Even walls and a roof. I checked earlier for you. We're surprisingly civilised out here in the wilds,' he said sarcastically.

She felt embarrassed and put a hand to her hot cheek.

'Don't be touchy. I just didn't know what to expect. The details didn't mention anything about electricity.'

He said nothing but led the way past a line of single-storey buildings, each with a little cluster of plants in clay pots outside. The buildings formed a square around a perfumed garden, which was a riot of double yellow jasmine, shoulder-high geraniums, oleander, almond blossom and magenta bougainvillaea.

'Oh, Khalil!' she cried in relief, turning happily to him. 'It's just perfect!'

He gave her a jaundiced look, grunted, and motioned sourly to a narrow doorway set in the rose-pink mud wall.

'They said it would be open,' she said uncertainly, but quite bubbling with excitement. The atmosphere here was peaceful and friendly. She felt immediately at home. It would make a good base—somewhere to relax after battling against Khalil every day.

He pushed open the door and they stepped into a tiny tiled area, open to the sky, an ornate wrought-iron dome over the opening above to protect any unwary children who might play on the roof. The simple rooms, each one half-tiled in cool blues, appeared to be set around the little courtyard, with a flight of stone steps leading to the roof.

'This is a typical Moroccan house,' said Khalil, opening every door in turn. 'Almost all are built around a central garden or yard, the only difference being that of size. You'll see exactly the same plan in the palace museum when we visit it.'

Hannah smiled contentedly, making a brief exploration while Khalil prowled along behind her after depositing the case in the double bedroom. She'd been relieved to discover that it had an ordinary bed with a duvet on it. The sitting-room was a mixture of East and West, sporting brightly coloured ottomans and low tables, Moroccan rugs and a television. However, when she reached the kitchen she came to a halt, frowning.

'Small, isn't it?' commented Khalil, unnervingly squeezing in behind her.

She hastily moved away and found herself immediately against the minuscule sink with its little draining-board. Apart from that, there was only a cooker and a tall, narrow cupboard filled with strong-smelling spices, some tinned food and dry goods. There wasn't space for anything else, apart from the chair beside the cooker. It certainly was basic. But what else did she need, in this climate? She smiled happily.

'I'll get you a fridge,' said Khalil. 'You can move the chair and put it there.'

'No, thank you,' she said stiffly, not wanting him to take over. This was her domain, the only place where she could be in complete charge. Marrakesh was his city, and she knew he'd make darn sure she realised that. She had to establish her own space somewhere. 'I'll get it myself.'

'What would you pay?' he asked.

'What?' She heaved a sigh of impatience. 'A bit lower than the price on it, I suppose.'

'Nothing is ever priced.'

'In that case, I'd go for a third of its value. That's how you bargain, isn't it?'

He shook his head. 'You have a lot to learn, Hannah. Go on like that and you'll never make a profit.'

'Well, what proportion do I pay then? A half? A quarter?'

'It's not a question of... Look, you'll have to trust me to show you. You don't honestly think bargaining is that simple? That everyone knows from the start that they have to work up to half the original price asked? Give us some credit, Hannah! We're not renowned throughout the world for our selling ability for nothing!'

'I do need you, don't I?' she said crossly.

'Yes. You do,' he answered, the velvet of his voice making the hairs on the back of her neck rise. She shivered and strained forwards to avoid the soft warmth of his breath.

'Mind the *tajine slaoui* under the sink,' he said, sounding amused. 'You'll be doing most of your cooking in that. You must try a lamb stew. I'll show you how to make it.'

'You?' She laughed, and then gripped the sink as a wave of dizziness came over her.

'Hannah——'

The concern in his voice and his hands on her shoulders were unbearable, but she needed him to hold her for a moment, she felt so odd. Though his powerful body, a hair's breadth away, made her head whirl even more and the thundering of her heart made her panic-stricken.

'I'm all right. I think it must be the travelling. And I've been so busy these past few days. Hardly any time to stop running. Hardly time to eat,' she said with a forced laugh. She didn't dare tell him she'd only just had her jabs. He'd dismiss her as a stupid blonde for sure.

His fingers moved slightly, massaging her arms, and she flinched as he touched the swollen one.

'Leave me alone!' she blurted out fiercely.

'Gently,' he said, taking two steps back so that he was back in the courtyard again. 'Shall I get some food sent in for your supper?' he asked, sounding pleased with himself.

All Hannah wanted was to be alone, so that she could lie down and let her mounting fever take its course.

'No. There's some rice here and a tin of tuna. I feel really tired and rather irritable. I'm on a very short fuse at the moment so you'll have to excuse me. I don't want much to eat, only to unpack and rest.'

'I'll be round in the morning, then,' he said cheerfully. 'I'll take you to the market and initiate you into the art of bargaining. I'll come at ten.'

Hannah struggled her way through a thick haze and a throbbing head. 'Ten,' she agreed faintly, wondering if she'd feel well enough. Perhaps after a night's sleep... If only he would *go*! 'Goodnight, Khalil,' she said a little desperately.

She turned away to the sink again, pretending to try the tap and realising with slight dismay that there was only cold water laid on. She heard Khalil bid her a quiet goodnight and his footsteps growing fainter.

Stumbling to the outer door she shut it firmly, turning the key in the lock, and made her way blindly to the bedroom by feeling her way around the wall of the courtyard.

But she didn't even have the energy now to undress. She'd expended too much, trying to maintain face in front of Khalil. Wearily pushing off her shoes, she attempted to remove her jacket. The hard throbbing in her arm made her cry out in agony when trying to slide off her sleeve.

Too ill to care, and reluctant to move her arm any more than she had to, she decided to sleep in her short-sleeved blouse and her skirt. In the morning she'd have a decent shower and would feel better. At least there was a water-heater for that.

She eased herself on to her right side. It was the only comfortable position she could find. Awful as she felt, there was some consolation in the fact that it hadn't been Khalil who had made her heart race, and caused her blood to flow hot and fast. It had been the effects of the injections.

She *was* immune to him, after all.

CHAPTER THREE

IT WAS a terrible night. She hardly slept, even though at one stage she crawled into the kitchen and tossed down a glass of Algerian wine she found—all there was in the bottle, otherwise she might have drunk more. Some of it slopped on to her shirt, staining it and made her groan with defeat. Unfortunately, it didn't help her to relax at all.

The night air was cold. Her body ached as if she had flu, the back of her head was sending shooting pains upwards and she dared not touch her left arm.

Yet towards morning she must have fallen into a deep sleep, because she woke to a hefty hammering on her front door. Gasping aloud with every movement as she rolled off the bed, she staggered dizzily across the courtyard, holding the back of her head in an attempt to stop the pain there.

'Hannah! Hannah! Are you all right?'

'Oh, for heaven's sake!' she yelled, a desperate note to her voice. 'I'm not ready, Khalil.'

She leaned against the wall, trying to pull herself together, the sun burning into the top of her scalp. The hammering continued and she moaned.

'Open the door!' he commanded. 'It's ten-thirty and I have appointments to keep.'

'Go away,' she cried miserably in a thick voice.

He took no notice. Finally she realised that the only way to stop his terrible pounding, which was making her feel hysterical, was to let him in. He'd see she was ill and leave her alone. Weakly she reached out shaking fingers and turned the key.

The door flew open. Khalil, dressed in a beautifully made cream *djellaba*, stood at the front of an interested sea of faces. He looked shocked. She blinked stupidly, licking her parched lips. The group of men behind him murmured. Khalil's eyes narrowed. He took one look at her and quickly stepped in, slamming the door behind him. Hannah winced.

'*Allah!* Just look at you!' seethed Khalil. His eyes strayed to the empty wine bottle, lying on its side by the kitchen door where Hannah had left it. 'My God! You still know how to hit the bottle, I see!'

Pain sliced her chest. He hadn't forgotten how to hurt her, or how to blister her with his anger. And it was always when she felt totally defenceless...

'Please! Don't yell!' she moaned, the words slightly slurred. She tilted back her head so that her hair flowed down her back in a tousled mass of shining gold. 'My head...'

Incapable of standing upright any longer, she clutched at the wall and slowly let herself slump to the ground. Khalil glared at her in frank disgust.

'An exhibitionist to the last. I ought to leave you to suffer,' he growled.

'Mmm. Go away,' she mumbled weakly, holding her head.

'And risk your neighbours discovering you're a drunkard?' he asked under his breath.

She heard a soft swish of cloth and he was bending over her, his arms reaching out to pick her up. She let out an involuntary gasp of pain as he touched her arm, but he swept her up nevertheless and strode into the bedroom. Briefly she burned with embarrassment as she felt the grip of his ruthless hands on her naked thighs where her skirt had ridden up, and then he was dumping her angrily on the bed, pushing back the duvet and thrusting her beneath. Hannah curled up miserably, wishing he'd leave.

'I'm not drunk,' she muttered.

'Oh? The stink of alcohol and the stain on your shirt is an illusion? You usually sleep in your clothes, do you?' he sneered.

'No. Only when I've got typhoid, or cholera,' she answered with sullen drama, needing sympathy, not disapproval. She hoped he felt like a heel. 'I had one gulp of wine and it spilt because my hand was shaky.'

'What?'

She flicked him a baleful glare. 'You heard. I'm ill, you insensitive swine. Touch my left arm again and I'll flatten you, weak as I am,' she croaked.

'By heaven...'

Khalil sat down cautiously on the bed beside her and stretched over, carefully lifting up her sleeve and seeing the pad of lint, the plaster holding it and the angry red flesh surrounding it.

'You stupid——! Why didn't you tell me, last night?'

'I just wanted you to go so I could be ill on my own,' she mumbled, feeling sorry for herself.

'Why...? If... Oh, hell!' He stared at her helplessly. 'You must feel awful,' he said, a variety of emotions seeming to be competing for room on his face.

She couldn't raise the energy to decide if he was angry, sympathetic or indifferent.

'I do. Terrible. Everything aches as if I'd gone fifteen rounds with Mike Tyson. And someone keeps cracking open the back of my head with an ice-pick. And I'm hot.' Fretfully, not thinking, she pushed down the duvet. Khalil covered her up again, frowning. 'I said, I'm hot!' she snapped, wrestling with it.

'I'm sure you are, but your blouse is unbuttoned and you're not wearing anything under it, are you? As well as that, your skirt has ridden up,' said Khalil sternly.

'Oh!' Her eyes rounded in alarm. One hand moved surreptitiously to see how much of her body he'd seen. Enough, she realised with horror, to know the extent of her swelling breasts. To remind him... Her eyes squeezed shut. Then they shot open again and she went bright red with an even greater humiliation. 'When I answered the door...'

She gulped, wondering if she'd made a terrible exhibition of herself, as he'd said. She'd never be able to face her neighbours again!

'You weren't too bad then. You looked dishevelled and probably made all of our pulses beat a little faster, and threatened the owner with cardiac arrest, but you weren't too indecent,' he said wryly.

'Oh, how ghastly,' she moaned, burying her face in the pillow in shame.

'You'll be OK tomorrow and can tell your neighbours all about it,' he said with a slight smile. 'Pity you don't look awful, as most women do when they're ill. Trust you to look beautifully abandoned.'

She looked at him with great suspicion, but there was no sarcasm in his face, only an odd, bemused expression. She wondered how many ill women he'd cared for, and was irritated to recognise the pangs of jealousy within her.

'I might have known you'd be an old hand at dishing out charm and medical advice to women. Done a lot of that, have you?' she asked crossly.

'I have ten brothers, all married, and five sisters,' he said, his eyes dark and intense. 'It's difficult not to know women, under those circumstances. Anyway, I do know that you need to rest and take plenty of liquids. Not alcohol. I'll get some fresh orange and settle you down, then I'll do a bit of shopping for you. You must eat.'

'Thank you,' she said meekly.

He smiled and, to Hannah's blurred, feverish mind, he looked like the gentle, charming Khalil she had once fallen in love with. Her heart skipped a beat and her blue eyes grew wistful. But it had all been in her imagination. When she blinked, she found that he was glaring at her coldly, his face tight and drawn.

'You ought to get out of your clothes,' he said shortly. 'You'll feel more comfortable.'

'I can't,' she said in a small voice. 'It hurts to use my arm.'

For several seconds he stared down at her, his expression inscrutable. 'Well, you'll have to put up with the discomfort, then,' he said. 'I'm certainly not undressing you.'

'It's not catching,' she said, a little petulantly.

His eyes glittered. 'What isn't catching, Hannah?'

'M-m-my reaction,' she stumbled, shaken by the soft velvet of his tone. His eyes had become strangely compelling. What was he up to? She plunged on, without thinking. 'I mean it would be all right if you touched me...' Her voice trailed away to nothing.

'Is that an invitation?' he asked, making her shake with the husky eroticism lacing his voice.

'Of course not,' she muttered, feeling contrary.

She longed to be free of her tight skirt and almost didn't care who removed it. Almost. The thought of Khalil's hands on her body made her tremble. Under the cover, she tried to ease the waistband and became increasingly frustrated at her lack of success. Every movement made her head spin and, to her astonishment, she found her eyes filling with helpless tears.

'I can't do it,' she said miserably. 'And I'm so hot...'

Khalil heaved a huge sigh. 'I don't know what it is about you,' he said angrily, sliding his hands under the duvet, 'but you seem incapable of living quietly and normally like everyone else. Your life is a series of dramas.'

His hands knew exactly what they were doing, even though they were working blind. Hannah felt resentful that he was so deft at undressing her. His experience must be phenomenal.

With a quick movement he undid the button on her waistband and slid down the zip, then, with a dark frown patterning his forehead, slipped his hands down her burning hot hips till they found the hem of her skirt. A quick yank and it was off, though not before his warm fingers had inadvertently travelled the length of her long legs and filled her with languor.

'That's cooler,' she said breathlessly, feeling the freshness of the sheet on her naked skin and wondering if he'd remove her blouse. For a moment she thought he intended to, and she lay motionless, waiting mesmerised, her hair spread out on the pillow, her eyes huge in her fevered face.

'I wouldn't imagine that many men have seen you in bed and walked away,' he said harshly, and did just that.

Hannah shrank into the mattress. It felt as if he'd thrown a bucket of cold water over her. Khalil thought she was so cheap that he could hardly bear to touch her, even though she lay there as a sick human being in need of help.

Indescribably miserable, she heard him moving about in the little kitchen. Then a jug of freshly squeezed orange juice was banged down on the table beside her and he made her sit up and drink. He dug a spoon into a honey jar and fed it to her as if she were a child, glaring all the time as she licked her sticky lips.

'What's the honey for, then?' she muttered. 'Hoping it'll sweeten me up?'

'You're past all hope of that. It was my mother's remedy for virtually everything,' he said, replacing the stopper in the honey jar.

'No sane woman ever questions a man's mother,' she said weakly.

He wasn't amused. Hannah wished she'd kept quiet.

'I'm going now. I'll lock you in for your own safety,' he said sternly. 'After your spectacular appearance at the door, I've no idea what kind of woman your neighbours think you are.'

Hannah opened her mouth to protest, but he'd slammed her bedroom door shut and left. She turned her face into the pillow with a groan. Her intention to show him what a calm, composed and capable woman she was hadn't even got off the ground. He hadn't actually said that she'd been a fool to leave her jabs so late, but he thought it, she could tell, from the way he had scowled at her. He despised her still. It all stemmed from that awful day when he'd thought she was drunk. It made her wince and blush with humiliation even now.

Her hazy mind began to wander back to that occasion when Khalil and half the world's Press had witnessed her apparent degradation.

But she was dragged back to the present, her heart jumping into her throat as she heard a voice calling. An Irish voice. It sounded like Dermot. A voice from the dead!

'Are ye all right now, Rapunzel?'

'Dermot?' she croaked. Her mind was unhinged by fever! She was talking to a ghost quoting fairy-tales.

There was a thud in the yard outside, and then a light tap on the bedroom door.

'Oim not after yer body,' said the voice. 'But that great hefty bloke left in an awful rage, an' a-slamming of doors, an' I was thinkin' you might be in trouble.'

Hannah felt her pulses slow. It wasn't Dermot—of course it wasn't! Only someone who sounded like him. But how had he got in? She checked that she looked vaguely respectable and called out huskily, 'Come in. Hello.'

He was unshaven, with a tousled mop of red hair, and was wearing a shapeless T-shirt and trousers he probably slept in. Yet his face was concerned and very friendly, and his accent alone made her warm to him.

'Hello yerself,' he said with a lopsided grin. 'I live next door. Patrick Murphy. Original, don't you think? There must be ten thousand Patrick Murphys in London alone, certain sure there must.'

Hannah giggled, then winced at the jarring of her head.

'Anythin' I can do?' asked Patrick uncertainly. 'I don't normally bust in on people, but I was a mite worried. Your boyfriend scared the hell out o' me.'

'He's a business colleague——'

'Ah. One of those. Sure, they're the worst.'

'Patrick, he is! He thought I was drunk and he disapproved. But I'm suffering from the after-effects of typhoid and cholera jabs. I'll be OK in a while. I'm Hannah Jordan.'

'Not Rapunzel? With that hair? Ah, well. You're a sight prettier than the twenty-stone Algerian who rented this place last. We took a vote outside on that just now.'

A smile crossed her face. 'How on earth did you get in? Khalil locked the door.'

'I know that. That's what worried me. I looked for your hair trailin' down the castle walls, but you'd forgotten to put it out to dry. So I went on my roof, jumped like a terrified gazelle over the wall between us, lifted up your grille and thudded down on to me own two flat feet. Was he locking you in, or locking us out?'

'The latter.' She grinned, her eyes twinkling. 'He thought I was in danger.'

'So you are. People have been known to submerge beneath the never-ending, open-handed offers of friendship in this country. Well, if you're OK——'

'Please don't go,' she begged. 'It's lovely, hearing your accent. I worked for someone who came from Cork, and it brings back memories.'

'Is that a fact? I'm a Bantry Bay man myself,' said Patrick, settling down. 'Confusing Moroccans and tourists alike with a nightly rendering of Irish folk-tunes in all the best hotels. What work do you do, then?'

'I used to be a secretary. Now I've started up a business and I'm here to do a bit of importing.'

'Ah, the James Bond touch. Import and Export—I've met a glamorous spy at last!'

Hannah lay against the pillows, listening with pleasure to Patrick's rapid chatter. He painted a slightly cynical but charming picture of her neighbours, and she felt cheered. He made them coffee and persuaded her to try some rather burnt cakes he'd baked.

After a while she began to feel a little better and Patrick was just leaning over her, helping her to sit up, when Khalil's voice made them both freeze.

'Well, you do make intimate friends easily, Hannah. Your hormones appear to work even when you're ill,' he drawled sarcastically.

'I doubt *you* have any friends at all,' she snapped, her eyes blazing defiance.

'Ah, the sound of lovers talking,' whispered Patrick in Hannah's astonished ear. Patrick straightened up and met Khalil's stern and steady challenge.

Hannah introduced them quickly. 'Patrick Murphy, meet Khalil ben Hrima,' she said with a sigh. Fate seemed to be determined to paint her as a harlot, entertaining men in bed.

'*That* Khalil!' cried Patrick. 'Sure, 'n I'm delighted to be meeting you. I thought you were locking up this lovely princess, so I dropped in from the heavens above to see if she wanted to be your prisoner. If you'd worn a label saying who you were, I wouldn't have bothered at all. Your honour and fame has spread, like the fat lady's hips.'

Khalil's mouth twitched, but Hannah wasn't too pleased to see Patrick's evident admiration for Khalil. She had thought the Irishman was on her side.

'You play in the Mamounia, don't you?' Khalil smiled. 'I like what you do.'

'T'anks. Do I have a vague recollection of seeing you there with a gorgeous young blonde?' asked Patrick. 'Or is that a secret?'

'You saw me,' said Khalil lazily, looking at Hannah's disapproving mouth. 'She's my niece.'

Patrick let out a guffaw of laughter and Hannah knew exactly what the blonde must look like by the expression on his face.

'Sure, I know the sort of niece you mean,' grinned Patrick, winking.

Khalil laughed wickedly. 'Look, I don't want to break this up, but...'

'Say no more,' said Patrick. 'T'ree's a crowd, as the tobacco plant in the pine forest said.'

Hannah laughed. 'Don't go——'

'I'm playing in the bar of the Mamounia any minute now.' Patrick grinned, patting Hannah's restraining hand. 'They'll not be able to drink their coffee without me. I'll be back to tell ye if they showered me with gold or sugar knobs. Till then.'

'He's nice,' said Hannah, when the bedroom door had closed.

'You're better,' countered Khalil, not commenting on Patrick.

'Improving every minute,' she answered brightly. 'Why did you come back?'

'I brought food. You ought to have an early lunch, since you had little to eat last night.'

'Oh. That's nice of you,' she said.

'It is, isn't it? Do you want to dress and tidy up, or have a snack in bed?' he asked abruptly.

She opted to get up, and spent a long time in the bathroom to the sound of chopping in the kitchen. As it was very warm, she put on a scoop-necked cotton dress in dazzling white.

On the roof, in the shade of the palms, she tucked into a salad he'd prepared and some well-spiced meat oozing from a sliced pocket in flat Berber bread. It *had* been a long time since she'd eaten, and she was starving. He sat cross-legged on a soft rug and she occupied the lounger, stretching out her long legs into the hot sun and munching on some honeyed almond pastries, her optimism and confidence almost restored.

'I really do feel a lot better,' she said. 'Thank you.'

'You're welcome.' His eyes regarded her thoughtfully. 'Take a rest now, though. If you feel up to it, we'll go to the *souk* this evening.'

'I want to explain about Dermot,' she said quietly.

A swift frown darkened his face. 'No. I've decided I don't want to hear. It was an unpleasant time for all of us and there's no point in turning over old ground.'

'Khalil——'

'No, Hannah!' he barked. 'Leave it. We'll take our relationship from today.'

'But if you persist in thinking I was Dermot's gold-digging mistress——'

'That's enough!' he said, his face stone-hard. 'The matter is closed.'

Hannah shrugged. He'd go to his grave disapproving of her, then. Showing she didn't care, she lay back on the lounger and shut her eyes. The warm sun filtered through the palm fronds and birds sang non-stop through the silence. The aroma of herbs and spices drifted to her nostrils, almost obliterating the heady scent of orange-blossom.

It had been weeks since she'd really relaxed, and she was very tired. Khalil was so quiet that her weary brain wasn't aware that he was still close. Her body grew inert and heavy, the languid afternoon spreading ahead of her. She flung one arm over her head, her mouth softening with half-sleep.

She smiled drowsily. A light breeze was flickering over her mouth, becoming warmer... Lazily her eyelashes lifted a fraction.

There was no breeze, after all, only Khalil's soft lips. His face was hovering over hers, his beautifully arched mouth descending again. Refusing to face reality, and still a little woozy, Hannah murmured her appreciation and closed her eyes, letting one arm rise to drape over his shoulder.

Half dreaming, she trailed her hand up to the nape of his neck, which was hot from the sun's rays. Gradually she increased the pressure till her fingers wound in his glossy hair and his kiss began that old familiar melting of every bone in her body. And then, to her utter dismay and sudden flash of shame, he unhooked her fingers and caught her shoulders in a bruising grip.

'Is this what you planned with Patrick, before I made my untimely entrance?' he asked quietly.

'Mmm? What?' she asked in confusion, her mouth full and ready still for kissing, her hand pressed to her thudding heart.

A muttered oath escaped his lips. He pushed aside her hand roughly and curved his palms around her voluptuous breasts, and, before she knew what was happening, had covered her mouth with his in a punishing kiss that never seemed to end.

She wanted it. Had hungered for it for years and years. So she couldn't deny him, or herself. It was as much a punishment for her as it was for him. They locked their bodies in anger and resentment, in futile, incomprehensible need. He lifted her from the lounger on to the rug and held her tightly, his hands tormenting her with their travels, arousing her more than she could bear.

'Khalil, no...' she began, with a valiant attempt to stop him.

'Hannah!'

He growled deep into her naked shoulder and his mouth ran hot over her flesh. She knew he was scarring her for life with his touch; that she'd never forget, nor would she ever want to. No wonder other men had meant nothing. Khalil meant all. Love, hate—whatever it was, she desired him with a passion that terrified her. Every slide of his teasing lips, every caress from his practised fingers, only served to enslave her. He, of all men, had the ability to make her forget everything but the pleasure of the moment, the delights he was arousing.

'Don't...' she whispered in desperation, cursing her memories.

He tipped up her chin and she foolishly opened her eyes to find herself falling, falling into those liquid, dark amber depths. Small moans erupted in her throat. Moans of need. He was shaking, hardly able to catch his breath, kissing her, telling her with his wrecker's eyes that he was her master and that he wanted her.

With a hard jolt, she was pulled into his body. The heat between them burned hotter than the sun on her back. His hands held her spine firmly, splaying out and ensuring that she didn't move. Then he slipped one hand away, sliding it insidiously to her hips and then, with slow, heart-stopping deliberation, higher and higher, back towards her defenceless breast.

She moistened her dry, bruised lips and found that they had been captured again, sweeping away her intended protest. A shudder ran through her, and then a deep, quivering gasp, as his fingers found the hard, aching bud beneath her dress which betrayed her secret desire.

'No,' she breathed, afraid of her wanton longing.

Khalil uttered a sound of pleasure in his throat that shook her to the core, echoing her joy as the exquisite sensations rocked through her body from the tip of her toes to the tingling hair on her head.

But he became still, his hand unmoving. Then he pushed her back to the ground, kneeling beside her, and she heard the call to prayer ringing out, harsh and plaintive, across the countryside.

'What a lot Patrick missed! Not a day goes by without your taking pleasure, does it?' breathed Khalil. 'Thanks to the *muezzin*, I am regretfully reminded of an appointment that I have this afternoon. As Dermot told me once, you have a startling ability to make one forget the tedious chores of everyday life. Excuse me. I'll call for you at seven. Dress soberly,' he growled, pulling up her dress where it had slipped from her shoulder. 'Neither I nor the men in the carpet co-operative will wish to mix sex with business.'

Hannah sat up, flushing at his cold tone. 'You attacked me while I was half asleep,' she accused. 'You manhandled me——'

'Oh, don't play games,' he snapped irritably. 'We're adults. We both knew what we were up to. Just damp down your passions for a while.'

'You cold-hearted, callous brute! Don't pretend to be immune,' she seethed. 'You weren't.'

He scowled. 'No, I wasn't,' he agreed. 'And later I'll take up your invitation and perhaps free myself from a few of the hang-ups I have about you.'

Hannah didn't like his menacing tone. 'What exactly do you mean by that?' she demanded warily.

His hand insultingly cupped her breast. 'We take up where we left off,' he said throatily, the promise in his eyes making her blood race. 'We should have been less inhibited years ago, Hannah. It might have solved all our problems.'

'I don't have any problems,' she breathed.

'You do now,' he said softly. 'From this moment on, you'll have to work out how you're going to stay awake all day if I keep you awake all night. Seven. We'll eat after. Then I'll take you home. And release a few repressions.'

'Khalil!' She jumped up as he made for the stairway down.

'Not now.' He grinned crookedly. 'Patience. The pleasure is in the waiting.'

Laughing mockingly at her open-mouthed look of astonishment, he ran down the stairs. In numb disbelief, she saw him glance briefly up at her from the courtyard below, and then, galvanised into action, she ran to the parapet wall, peering over, trying to attract his attention as he strode lithely to his car. With a sense of despair, she saw him reverse and drive away without another look in her direction.

Shaking uncontrollably, Hannah sought a diversion from her whirling brain and made herself a cup of mint tea, glaring at the sound of the *muezzin*, who was still calling the faithful to prayer. It had happened again. Her loving heart had betrayed her.

The men she loved seemed destined to use her. Dermot had, to some extent. Now Khalil. For she was under no illusion: the love she felt for Khalil had erupted again.

It was still powerful and obsessive, and would probably destroy her if she allowed it to.

Destruction had almost overcome her once before, when she was eighteen and Khalil had abandoned her. Looking back on it, she could see that to him it must have been a brief, pleasant flirtation. Living in a fool's paradise, she had imagined that the depth of their passion meant that they loved each other, despite their short time together. She'd been wrong, of course, otherwise he wouldn't have stayed away for four whole years.

When he had returned to Dermot's manor-house in southern Ireland, two years ago, it hadn't even been to renew their affair. He'd merely come because of the adverse publicity. There'd been a spate of scurrilous newspaper reports about her relationship with Dermot, and some embarrassing photographs of revellers at the never-ending parties in the manor.

She had resisted the idea of the parties to begin with, but Dermot had needed them. 'I'm afraid of dying,' Dermot had told her. 'Keep me alive, Hannah, with music and dancing. Fill the house with laughter.'

'You need peace and quiet, Dermot——' she'd protested.

'I want to leave this world grinning,' he'd said querulously. 'Not in solemn silence. Please—I don't have long, we both know that. Put a brave face on it, don't let anyone know I'm terrified, Hannah. Help me to forget.'

How could she deny him? Yet she was exhausted. Each day she typed out streams of words as Dermot dictated, lying on his couch. All the time she tried to be bright, witty and sparkling for him. Later she would preside at dinner, coping on her own with Dermot's wild and occasionally wicked guests. He was draining her of life, but she loved him and knew he had to finish his book. He was a genius. It was vitally important.

Khalil walked in, unannounced, in the middle of dinner, as a Welsh film actor was relating a particularly questionable story. Her heart turned over, as if Khalil had never left. If he called, she would go. If he smiled, her world would turn again.

He blocked the doorway with his bulk, dominating the room. His merciless eyes were like narrow lasers which chilled her, inch by inch. Suddenly Hannah felt tawdry in the glitzy, revealing dress which Dermot had so admired and asked her to wear that evening.

'A word,' commanded Khalil, not moving from the doorway.

Like a fool, she'd gone to him, hoping to gain his approval again. But, to hide her eagerness, she rose as if she was a cool, composed hostess, challenging him with her own frostiness. In her heart she knew there was no hope really—though maybe she'd discover why that should be.

'I've been up to see Dermot. He looks terrible,' he said grimly, when they were alone in the study.

'Is that all you have to say, after all this time?' she asked quietly.

'I've stayed away because I couldn't bear to see my stepfather making himself look stupid by running after a cheap, mercenary floozie,' he growled.

Her eyes hardened, and her breast rose in anger. 'You don't believe what you read in the Press, surely?' she asked heatedly. 'You know it's pure sensationalism. They love to think of Dermot as another Hemingway.'

'You haven't denied any of it. I see no protests, no court actions defending your good name.'

She shook her head in exasperation. 'Dermot consulted his lawyers and they said any action would be expensive and pointless.'

'Are you sure he did that?' asked Khalil, his eyes baleful.

She bristled. 'I hope you're not calling him a liar.'

Khalil lifted a cynical eyebrow. 'He's Irish and a writer. He rearranges the truth.'

'Why should he?' She frowned in annoyance. 'Besides, fighting the Press would take time away from writing, and he needs every hour he can manage. He says to let them all think what they like, and to hell with them. They'll go and pester someone else eventually. I'm too busy to keep issuing writs. Their lies don't touch me—I rise above it all.'

'Or beneath it. You're killing him with your excesses,' he said, his eyes pure jet. 'I've come to ask you to leave him.'

'No!' she said vigorously. 'I couldn't do that. Over the least few years he's come to rely on me totally.'

'Clever,' sneered Khalil. 'I suppose he's made his will in your favour——'

'Of course he hasn't!' She caught hold of his arm and he scowled ferociously, but didn't push her away. 'Khalil, if I'd known you'd stayed away because *you* thought I was his mistress——'

'I knew that was your true role when I first met you, and you were just eighteen,' he breathed. 'I thought then I might persuade you to leave him and come back with me to Marrakesh. Watching you writhe around in the meadows beneath me was playing havoc with my pulse-rate.'

Her heart lurched. 'What stopped you from asking?'

He gestured to her finger. 'Dermot gave you that emerald ring and I could see from your greedy face that you knew perfectly well which of us to stay with. I had little money then, after all. What I heard later confirmed my suspicions.'

'How can you mistake greed for joy?' she said heatedly. 'I was thrilled. That gift meant a lot to me,

more than you know. It was my birthday, and that was
the first birthday present I'd ever had.'

'Would you have left?' he asked savagely, catching
hold of her and shaking her till her teeth rattled. 'Answer
me! Would you?'

'No! I wouldn't!' she yelled. 'Dermot needed me. I've
never been needed before! I couldn't leave him. I——'
She bit her lip. She'd sworn never to tell anyone that
Dermot was terminally ill.

He gazed down at her, his face a mixture of exasperation and... Hannah's lips parted. Was that despair?
Pain flooded her eyes. Did he still desire her? Khalil lifted
his hand to touch her hair.

'Hannah——' He broke off at the sound of a tinkling
bell and his hand fell lifeless to his side.

'That's him,' she said, relieved, knowing she'd been
about to make a fool of herself and run after Khalil
again. 'I must go. He'll be in bed, wanting me to chat.'

'Go to your lover,' growled Khalil bitterly.

'You're jealous,' she accused scathingly. 'He hinted
that you were. You envy the close relationship between
us, don't you?'

Khalil's dark eyes brooded on her. 'You grasping
bitch! Can't you see he's using *you*?' He laughed, but
the laughter didn't reach his eyes. His hand whipped out
and caught her chin. 'You look terrible beneath that thick
make-up. Your eyes are hollow. Dissipation is setting in,
Hannah. Dermot is a true, selfish genius. He devours
people to give himself life. And you think you're using
him! Huh! He's a past master at manipulation.'

She dragged herself away, shaking with anger. 'Sour
grapes!' she retaliated. 'You don't have a shred of cre-
ative ability and don't understand him. This house has
to pivot around him. I'm giving him everything he wants
and I'm willing to make that sacrifice, whatever it does
to me.'

'Everything?' he thundered.

The little bell dinned into her senses. She ran out. She couldn't tell him why she was devoting this part of her life to Dermot. Khalil obviously had his suspicions, but they mustn't be confirmed. Those were Dermot's orders. She had to protect him and not let him become agitated.

Tired and subdued, she spent a long time reading to Dermot because he seemed rather vulnerable and needed gentle attention. She had returned to her own room and undressed, when she heard him call her name.

'Throw open the windows, Hannah,' he said quietly, when she came in through the interconnecting door. 'Tonight I want to see the stars.'

'There's a lovely bright moon,' she said, drawing back the curtains and unlatching the floor-length windows.

Silver light flooded into the room, catching the satin sheen of her négligé in a pale glimmer. From Dermot's bedroom in the front of the house she could see clearly up to Khalil's balcony, which was on the west wing, jutting out at an angle to the main building. His room was in darkness. He must be asleep.

'Thank you for what you've done for me,' said Dermot weakly.

She whirled at his sad tone, forcing a bright smile to her face. 'We're both having fun, aren't we?' she said cheerfully.

'You don't regret spending four years of your life with me?'

'Absolutely not,' she answered with vigour. His was the only love she was likely to know for a while. She couldn't see herself falling for anyone half as compelling as Khalil. 'I get reflected glory. Not every girl has a famous author for a father.'

'Oh, you like fame. So that's the reason you stay.' He smiled faintly, both of them knowing full well that it wasn't. He beckoned her over. 'I'm cold,' he said, shivering. 'Frightened.'

Hannah sat on the bed and put her arms around the frail body, which was normally disguised by day with layers of clothes. 'Keep punching,' she urged. 'Up off the canvas, you old fraud. You've only reached round four.'

He laughed, then coughed and rolled back on to the pillow, pulling Hannah with him. She stayed motionless till he'd stopped shaking and coughing, then she extricated herself slowly and gently.

After settling him for the night she went back to her own bedroom, feeling very sad. Sometimes she longed for someone to lean on, to pour out her problems to. Letters to her friend Frankie helped, but...

Hannah stopped herself drifting into wishful thinking. The house was quiet. Weary, she slept heavily. In the early hours she was woken by the brightness of the moonlight shining on her face. She rose to shut her curtains and, looking up, she saw Khalil on his balcony dressed only in a pair of jeans and pacing up and down, the moon making every moving muscle on his tanned torso gleam and bewitch her.

She wanted him to wrap her in his arms and comfort her, to take over the intolerable burden of daily cheerfulness, the effort of amusing Dermot's friends when he slipped away, pretending he had to write. She needed Khalil and his strength; the gentle, courteous wisdom he'd once freely shared with her. No longer could she cope alone. She'd reached the end of her tether.

Khalil seemed to feel her burning gaze. He looked down. Their unguarded eyes met, locked, and parted. He spun on his heel and went inside and left a void within her.

And yet, a few moments later, there was a knock outside. Hastily, joy and apprehension making every nerve flutter, she flung on her wrap and opened her bedroom door.

'Khalil——' She stopped at the fury on his face.

'You bitch! I've been unable to sleep because of you. I can't stand it any longer,' he said harshly. 'I saw you in Dermot's bed, forcing your beautiful body on him. How could you! How can you do this! He's fifty-one, Hannah, and you're young and lovely. Stop living like this, or...'

Misery engulfed her. She felt more lonely, more tired and rejected than ever before. It wasn't worth arguing with him. What he was saying was too ludicrous for words. The doors to her heart were locked again.

'Or what?' she asked, her eyes huge and moist. 'What can you do to me?'

He was shaking with anger. He swept one contemptuous glance over her beautiful pale pink satin négligé. Her breathing was heavy, making her breasts rise and fall. Khalil seemed to explode. Before she could stop him, he had pushed his way past her, had kicked the door shut and had caught her in his arms, jerking her against his naked chest.

'I loathe you! But I can make you forget money, forget your cold-hearted desire to dig for gold,' he grated.

'Let me go!' she said in a hoarse whisper, arching backwards. 'You'll wake Dermot.'

'I don't give a damn!' he said thickly. 'Even if this makes me despise myself for the rest of my life, I'm not hiding my feelings any more. Tonight I'm having what I want and maybe you'll discover it's what you want, too.'

'No——'

Terrified as to his intentions, his fierce grip crushing her body, she stared wide-eyed at his darkening expression.

'Oh, Hannah!' he whispered brokenly.

Her heart seemed to stop. Somehow they fused as if they'd never been apart, their kisses raining on each other like welcome showers in the desert. His lips were burning, his passion undeniable. He bent her supple body to his will and she revelled in his strength. Heat welled up between them, liquefying their bodies till they seemed to be floating.

The bitterness and the misunderstandings were over. He would care for her. They could love again.

'Let me touch you,' he whispered, loosening the braided ribbon of her négligé.

Desperately needing physical contact, the comfort of his touch after years of selfless sacrifice, Hannah was suspended in a dream, one she'd lived hopelessly for so long that she couldn't halt it now that it had become real.

Her robe fell open, and his hands ran in wonder over the smooth satin of her nightdress beneath. His hands caressed her, revelling in the feel of the slide of satin cloth over satin skin. He learned the shape of her body through his fingertips and she groaned as every part of her became sensitised and alive.

'You're beautiful,' he said huskily, a slight catch in his voice.

As if she'd been born for this moment, Hannah smiled dreamily and raised her arms, drawing him to her. His mouth ran over her body, slowly, surely, making her tremble and feel as if she were afire with energy.

'If only I didn't hate you,' he whispered.

'Khalil!' she cried in shock. Her body became suddenly rigid.

His fingers trailed possessively over her mouth. 'Come away with me,' he urged. 'You have to leave Dermot.'

'No! I can't!' she breathed, her throat dry with horror.

She had projected her own love on to Khalil in her desperate need for affection. But his motive in kissing her had been low, carnal and despicable. He needed only sexual satisfaction.

'Yes! I want you!' he said savagely.

He jerked her back against him with one quick, rough movement. His kiss was violent in its desperation and she forced her head to stay clear as her body demanded that she surrender to his overwhelming hunger. But he hated her—he wanted to possess her in order to separate her from a dying man.

With a supreme effort, she wriggled her hands up to his shoulders and pushed hard. He rocked with the force of her sudden movement and then they both froze at the quavering cry coming from Dermot's room.

'Nerma! Dear God in heaven! Forgive me!'

'Dear Allah!' cried Khalil, racing in.

Broken, she leaned her head against the wall, knowing instinctively what had happened. It had all ended.

A sob escaped from her trembling lips. There was nothing she could do for Dermot now. He hadn't even called her name, she thought miserably, but that of the main character in his first blockbuster which had rocketed him to fame. She didn't want to see him, not now, only to remember him at his best, when he'd been alive.

From then on, ignoring her totally, Khalil coped with everything. She couldn't cry. Her face remained a cool mask. For everything she had loved had gone that terrible night, and her emotions had gone, too. The route to her heart had been cut off.

Reporters and cameramen besieged the house. Empty and rudderless again, moving in a mechanical unreality, she didn't demur when the doctor gave her some tranquillisers to cope with the funeral, nor when the housekeeper insisted that she drink some brandy. After being in charge for so long, it was a welcome change to be free of decision-making. The brandy made her feel very peculiar.

The Press were awful, turning the whole ceremony into a three-ring circus. Their attention was concentrated on her, much to Khalil's tight-lipped disapproval, as they asked her to pose for them: the beautiful young woman who'd loved a literary legend.

At the graveside service she clutched a single red rose, and tried to throw it on Dermot's coffin, but she stumbled and almost fell, gasping as Khalil's arms saved her and their faces collided. A dozen cameras flashed.

'You drunken slut!' hissed Khalil, recoiling at her breath on his cheek.

She lashed out at him blindly, struggling. 'How dare you?' she raged, hysteria rising as she found herself held by him. 'What do you know about me? What——'

'Keep your voice down,' he growled in her ear, holding her tightly. 'I know you've been drinking and we all know your reputation. The reporters are laying bets on your next Sugar Daddy. Besides, I saw you with Dermot, remember. He told me himself what you were. May Allah curse you, Hannah, for what you've done to me!'

'Let me go!' she cried vehemently, trying to hide her face from the sudden blinding flash-bulbs as reporters elbowed aside the mourners and scuffles broke out at the graveside. 'Khalil, please!' she wailed. 'I can't bear this!'

'You can't bear it?' he seethed. 'What about him? You killed him! You deliberately exhausted him with your young body, with sex and parties and booze——'

'No!' she yelled, beyond herself. 'I loved him! I really loved him! I——'

Khalil had gone. She collapsed to the ground in a blinding battery of flashes. She made headlines. The story ran every day for a week, with a new angle, a new 'revelation' each day. Someone said that Khalil had been seen talking to the journalists.

Hannah had to learn to harden herself to it, or go under. She fled to sanctuary in the anonymity of London with Frankie, her dearest friend, and licked her wounds.

Dermot's estate went to Cancer Research, as she'd known it would. She inherited one emerald ring, bittersweet memories, and the undying hatred of the second man she had loved in her life. Khalil.

CHAPTER FOUR

HANNAH rose decisively from her chair in the little Marrakesh house where she'd been daydreaming. Tonight, when he picked her up for her first trip to the *souk*, he'd find her strong again. She'd been through hell and had grown a new skin over the burns.

The kiss that afternoon on the roof-top had been an accident. He'd taken advantage of her temporary weakness. He'd shown her before that he lusted after her. She must be careful.

He wasn't to be blamed. She'd gone into the embrace wholeheartedly enough, so there was no point in feeling bitter because he'd jumped at the opportunity. He was like all the other men: after anything he could get. He'd learn. He'd find that she wasn't to be seduced or bullied into bed. All the other men who'd tried had conceded defeat, eventually.

It was just a pity that they were going to be thrown into each other's company so much over the next two months, and that she had to rely on him to guide her on her buying spree.

Her record of withstanding Khalil's advances hadn't been very good, up to now. She'd need to make him dislike her, otherwise he'd take the first opportunity to make love to her and destroy all her hard-won self-respect. He hated brash, extrovert women. She was determined to be just that.

So, looking brash, and determined to be breezy again, Hannah was delighted by Khalil's startled reaction to her when he called. Her years of hiding her feelings and being cheerful for Dermot were coming in useful.

He'd begun by greeting her with hungry eyes, as if he was contemplating his proposed night of seduction.

'How beautiful you look. Are you ready for me?' he'd murmured, leaning nonchalantly against the door-jamb.

'Absolutely. Every glorious inch is on Red Alert,' she'd replied expansively, imagining that his English wouldn't be up to that.

He examined her glorious inches carefully, by the light of the lamp hanging above her doorway, a mocking smile on his face.

Needing a morale-booster, she'd decided to wear a colourful Indian silk skirt and high-necked, embroidered mint-green blouse which flowed easily over her breasts and skimmed dramatically into her small waist. Her hair tumbled about her shoulders, untamed. She looked good, she felt good. And cold. And tough.

'Red Alert, you say? I see no state of alarm,' he said drily.

Hannah arched her brow. 'Oh, I'm not nervous of you. No, I meant I was just in a state of high awareness.'

'Me, too,' he drawled. 'I'm glad you've decided to be your true self.'

'You should have let me finish,' she said sweetly. 'I was going to say that I'm ready for anything. Especially to defend anyone or anything that interferes with my aims.'

'I was hoping that your aims were the same as mine,' he retorted smoothly.

She fixed him with a steady gaze. 'Somehow, I think not. I don't want to waste time parrying passes, Khalil,' she said brusquely. 'I have one goal only. I intend to make my *Souk Moroccaine* the most talked-about place in London—and a humdinger of a tourist attraction. No one is going to hold me back now.'

'Meaning that Dermot held you back?' he queried.

'No, of course not. He taught me a lot.'

'I'll bet he did,' he said, folding his arms. 'He took away your innocence and showed you how to enjoy debauchery.'

'My, what a lot of unusual words you know,' she scathed.

'I learnt that one from you,' he muttered. 'Or, at least, from a newspaper report about you.'

'No doubt it was one you supplied the details for. Shall we go?' she asked lightly. 'I'm eager to clinch a few deals and make a profit as soon as possible.'

'I admire ambition. But it can be a bit blind to other delights. Take care that you don't miss something interesting on your way up the ladder.'

'Ladders are old-fashioned. I use express lifts. I've seen nothing to entice me into other departments yet,' she said. 'But I'll let you know if I do. Tell me, though, because I *am* interested: where did you buy that gorgeous robe? I'd like to import some like that. I can see half of Kensington reclining in them, reading the Sunday newspapers. It really does things for you,' she said enthusiastically, arching saucy eyebrows and playfully patting his chest. Attack was better than defence. He might as well know that she felt confident about touching him and about handling the situation.

He drew in his breath and beneath her lingering fingers his ribcage swelled dangerously beneath the pure white *djellaba*, in a soft thin wool, and which was exquisitely braided on every seam. She avoided mentioning that there must be a thousand tiny buttons down the front; he'd only suggest that she started undoing them now, to save time later!

'I had it made. I'll make enquiries about bulk orders,' he said curtly. 'You seem very bouncy. You've recovered remarkably quickly.'

A brilliant grin flooding her face, she flung him a casual shrug. 'I always do,' she said perkily. 'Nothing gets me down for long. I spring back like trodden grass.'

'Hmm. That's either because you've developed an immunity to careless feet, or because you're made entirely of synthetics,' he commented, his mouth grim.

'Both,' she laughed.

'I thought so,' he muttered. 'Shall we go?'

'Will I need something to keep me warm?' she asked, wide-eyed.

He looked at her sourly for a few seconds before giving an imperceptible nod of his head.

'It'll get colder as the evening goes on.'

'Yes,' she said in a patronising tone. 'I intend it to.'

Hannah threw a thick Indian shawl over her shoulders and was just getting into Khalil's car when she saw Patrick, who was emerging from his house for his evening's work. She cheekily blew him a kiss.

'Any bags of gold thrown at you last night?' she asked him, with a grin.

'Enough to buy us lunch tomorrow, Rapunzel, if the witch will let you out of your tower,' he joked. 'Hello, Khalil. How's yerself?'

'Busy,' he replied curtly.

'Patrick, if I've any problems with the witch, I'll let my hair down for you,' promised Hannah. 'One o'clock tomorrow, then? We'll be finished our morning's work by then, won't we?' she said, turning to Khalil.

He nodded, his face inscrutable.

'Do I dress casually, or dress to kill?' she called out to Patrick.

'Sure, you can come in nothing at all, it's all the same by me.' He shrugged, with a deceptively innocent look.

Her reply was prevented by the sudden roar of the engine. Incapable of making herself heard, and rather pleased that Khalil was so annoyed, she waved vigorously to Patrick as Khalil concentrated on reversing the car down the unlit dirt track.

'Isn't life fun?' she enthused. 'I love Irishmen.'

'So I gather,' he responded bitingly.

Hannah suppressed an inner giggle. She'd chosen the right response to Khalil. He couldn't cope with dominant women who said what they thought and blissfully ignored his sexual harassment.

'I've been looking forward to this evening enormously,' she said smugly, teasing him.

'Oh?' he said cautiously. 'Why?'

'The cut and thrust of business, of course. What else? I adore it. I'm dying to get my teeth into a bit of commerce.'

Khalil turned on to the main road.

'It'll make a change from sinking them into me,' he said drily.

'Steady,' she warned, grinning. 'There's an increasing danger that you might say something amusing.'

'Is that all life is to you?' he asked sourly.

Hannah felt elated, the more gloomy he became. She was well able to hold her own. No longer were her emotions in danger.

'What else is life about?' she exaggerated. 'Dermot said—— '

'Damn Dermot!' he thundered. 'Spare me! I don't want to hear his little homilies. I've read the books. They were brilliantly written but were based on half-understood facts. I've seen the interviews. They were very entertaining and showed everyone that he was one hell of a guy, but he was a fraud, really, wasn't he?'

'How dare you say that!' exclaimed Hannah hotly. 'He was worth ten of you, any day.'

'He was a single-minded, selfish man who deliberately created an image for himself and hid behind it.'

'You're jealous!' she cried, not liking his perception.

'We seem to be arguing again,' murmured Khalil.

'We——'

To her annoyance, he was right. Hannah discovered that she was leaning forward tensely, ready for battle. She subsided again with irritation. He'd broken through her poise and cheerfulness without even seeming to try! And from the way he was smirking, he'd meant to rile her. Infuriating man!

'I just don't like you to get away with stupid remarks,' she said sweetly. 'All right, we don't mention Dermot again, since you're obviously so jealous of his talent. No,' she said as he opened his mouth to say something, 'we'll stick to business. Yes?'

'For the time being,' he agreed softly, shooting her a menacing glance. 'Just for the time being.'

There was silence for a moment as they both tried to regain their composure. After a little while they entered the Bab Nkob, eerily lit against the solidity of the black night sky. Soon they came upon the open space which Hannah knew—from the guidebooks—must be the Djemaa el-Fna.

It was a market-place, yet like no other in the world. She was instantly fired by its glamorous, colourful bustle and the exotic African pageantry parading before her eyes. Her exuberance increased with every second, making her face glow with radiance.

The brooding Khalil parked opposite the improbable-sounding Café de France, and gave a few coins to a child to look after the car. Then he motioned for Hannah to follow him. The air hummed with sound. To her disappointment they walked right past the stalls, the snake charmers and the musicians. Crowds were gathered around the various performers in circles, each circle merging with another so that the whole square coiled and seethed with life. High into the black velvet sky a troupe of acrobats towered, balancing precariously, a young boy working beneath them and accepting coins from the hands of awed watchers.

'What a lot of different kinds of people are here!' she commented to Khalil, catching his arm to slow him down.

He glanced around and motioned to various groups. 'They're Saharan nomads. Those, negroes from the far south . . . and Jews . . . and pure Arabs. The light-skinned men are Berbers: the original inhabitants of Morocco, before the Arabs came.'

He moved on and they eased their way with difficulty through the throng. All around was a low rumble of voices, the sound of rhythmic drums and laughter from the people watching the clowns. The bells of the gaudily dressed water-sellers mingled with the loud and dramatic tones of the storytellers, who were holding huge audiences enthralled.

'How many people are here, do you think?' she asked.

'Must be nearly fifteen thousand. Stay close.'

The astonishing thing was that this wasn't staged for tourists. Nearly all the people in the huge square were Moroccans, going about their daily business. Or nightly business, rather. And the majority were men, the women probably remaining behind locked doors, she thought. It wasn't a woman's world. No wonder she was being stared at.

'Can't we stop?' asked Hannah hopefully.

'No, this isn't a guided tour,' he said heartlessly, throwing her a quick glance over his shoulder.

And then, without warning, his hand caught her wrist and she was hauled roughly against his body, slamming into him with a thud. Stunned and outraged, she opened her mouth to say something and saw a sheet of flame pass by her face. She clutched at Khalil's chest and found he was yelling furiously—but not at her. Cautiously she followed his blazing eyes and saw a half-naked fire-eater, waving a torch around and yelling back.

'Are you all right?' asked Khalil curtly, looking down on her.

'A little hot under the collar, perhaps,' she joked, thinking how solid he felt. Dependable. Odd, how one's physical responses had no common sense at all. He was about as dependable as the English weather.

He seemed reluctant to let her go.

'The man says he was jostled, but I could report him for dangerous practice, if you wish.'

Khalil's voice was vibrating deep within his chest. Hannah's fingers tingled. 'Please don't,' she said shortly.

'How appropriate that the flames of fire should bring us together,' he murmured.

'I'll report you for dangerous practice,' she said calmly.

With a grunt, he released her and moved on, strolling into a narrow alley the width of his shoulders.

Hannah endeavoured to keep up with him as he wove in and out of the crowds buying, selling, bartering, exhibiting, gossiping. His height kept him in view, above red fezes, blue turbans, black skull-caps and the white cotton head-dresses belonging to men from the Rif mountains.

People jostled her, elbowing, pushing, shoving. Once she could have sworn that someone pressed deliberately against her back when she was jammed up against a donkey, laden with hides and bound for the tannery. Her hands had been clapped to her nose at the smell, and a body briefly heated her entire spine before melting away into the crowd again.

'Khalil!' she cried, startled. Then, annoyed with herself, she whipped around to see if anyone had a guilty look. She'd get Khalil to give the man the rough edge of his tongue!

'Trouble?'

'One of your opportunist friends,' she said scathingly. 'Trying to find out if I'm wearing any underwear.'

Khalil's head jerked around as he glared with glittering eyes at the crowds surrounding them. 'Where?' he rasped, sounding furious.

'*Balek!*' came a cry behind her.

Khalil pulled her roughly to his chest, out of the way. 'Make way for donkeys,' he muttered.

She caught the tantalising, musky scent of his body and every nerve within her leapt into life.

'There's a joke in there somewhere, if I could only think of it,' she said brightly.

'I think you may be right,' he smiled wryly. 'The world is full of donkeys.'

And she was one, she thought, to find Khalil so exciting to be near. There was no reason why she should be thrilled when he touched her. She knew perfectly well that he was doing it deliberately. All she had to do was let him know that he did nothing for her. Nothing at all.

'Never mind,' she said, patting his chest sympathetically. 'You're in good company.'

He laughed into her eyes and it was all she could do to stop herself responding. It seemed like an eternity before he released her and she could ease the fixed, teasing expression on her face.

They sauntered on without hurrying, though not slowly enough for Hannah, who longed to stop and examine everything in her own good time, but the maze of alleyways confused her totally and she knew that she was dependent on Khalil for the moment. On another day she'd come back and look at the pottery, the stalls laden with bolts of cloth, pointed leather slippers and sweets. It would be fascinating to wander on her own, and she'd take care to wear something armour-plated.

'This is the *Criée Berbère*,' said Khalil, stopping briefly to wave his arm at an area ahead festooned with rugs and carpets. 'The old slave-market. It operated till quite recently. Come in here, first.'

They entered a narrow open doorway hung with rugs on every side, no different from the others. It would be impossible to find again, she thought.

'Khalil!'

He was immediately embraced by a huge bearded man with a booming voice. Hannah wondered if this was one of his relations and Khalil was making sure all the business she did was kept in the family.

'Miss Hannah Jordan,' he said, introducing her.

'You are welcome to Morocco, to Marrakesh, to the Great Friday Carpet House,' said the man, greeting her enthusiastically.

'Well, thank you,' grinned Hannah, as he placed his hand on his chest in a gesture of heartfelt meaning.

Before them was a vast tiled room with a high ceiling set with ornate coloured glass. The sides of the room were stacked high with folded carpets, while others hung suspended from the ceiling—some ten or twelve feet long. Hannah's eyes sparkled. This was going to be fun.

'Please, to sit,' said the man who'd welcomed them, with a gracious gesture. He pointed to a richly damasked ottoman, and she was about to accept the invitation when Khalil beat her to it, settling himself and lounging comfortably like an oriental potentate.

'And for you,' smiled the man, pointing to a seat set lower than Khalil's.

'Equality?' she murmured to Khalil.

He leaned over and put his mouth close to her ear. 'I am an old and valued customer and friend. You are, as yet,' he chuckled softly, 'untried.'

Hannah smiled faintly and stood up, aware that Khalil's amused eyes were on her. Two young men came to fuss over Khalil, acting very deferentially, and she thought sourly how much he loved to lord it over people. She ignored him, reaching out and feeling one of the huge hanks of wool hanging above her head.

'They use henna to dye the wool red,' said Khalil.

'Really?' she said, fascinated. 'And the others?'

'Saffron for yellow, indigo for blue, kohl for the black and mint for green. All natural dyes. There are others, of course.'

'Perhaps you'd give me a list,' she said eagerly, waving her expressive hands. 'Our customers will be *riveted*.'

Khalil flicked her a suspicious glance from under his thick lashes. 'Are you mocking me?' he asked tightly.

Her eyes rounded in astonishment. 'No, of course not! It's thrilling, isn't it?'

'Yes,' he said slowly, considering her vibrant face. 'I suppose I have to admit that it is.'

The man began to unfold carpets on the floor in front of them and young boys leapt to hold up one end for her approval, so she could see the shading. The carpets were beautiful and Hannah happily imagined them hanging beneath the decorated arcades in her London market.

'Are these all genuine?' she asked Khalil contentedly.

'Yes,' said the big bearded man, hearing her and pulling a strand from one of the fringes edging a carpet. 'Not plastic. You burn. See.'

She laughed and the man beamed. Khalil struck a match, smiling, and lit the end of the strand.

'Smell,' he said.

'What for?' she asked, sniffing in the burning wool.

Khalil said something and the man brought him another piece of wool, which was also lit.

'It's acidic,' she declared, wrinkling her nose and drawing back from the smouldering strand.

'Now you know how to tell the genuine from the fake,' said Khalil.

'I wish all judgements could be that simple,' she mused.

'So do I, Hannah. It would save us a lot of heartache, wouldn't it?' he said quietly.

She stiffened at the meaning in his tone. But, just then, one of the young boys gave a cry of dismay and hurried over. To Hannah's astonishment, he adjusted the vase of soft pink rose-buds on the table so that the flowers faced her.

She put her hand on the boy's arm. 'Thank you,' she smiled. 'You're very kind. Er . . . *merci*.'

She was rewarded by a beaming grin and a flood of Arabic and French.

'He apologises that no one noticed before,' translated Khalil. 'Beautiful flowers should look at one another. He means you,' he said wryly.

'Are you serious?' she asked. 'Or is that abject flattery? Do they know I might be a big customer?'

'No. They know only that you are with me,' he answered. 'They'd do the same for any woman, even one not as . . . beautiful as you.' Hannah blushed. 'More like a rose every minute,' he mocked. 'Oh, I'm not typical, Hannah. Don't judge my countrymen by my cynicism. There are those, as you've noticed, who will try to take advantage of you, as there are anywhere in the world. But it is in our nature to be considerate, thoughtful and courteous. You'll notice that, frequently. Don't take my word for it. Thoughtfulness is so much a part of everyday life for me that I forget it comes as a shock to you uncivilised British,' he added with a challenging look.

Hannah was too charmed by the boy's behaviour to let his sharp tongue irritate her. 'Olde-worlde courtesy,' she mused. 'How nice.'

'Now,' he said, turning to the carpets before them and pointing to different ones. 'Which of these do you like? You recognise the kilims, I'm sure. Then those large, formal ones are called Kingdom carpets, those are silk and wool, these are Chichaoua, these Glaoui.'

'I'd want selections of all of them in our shop,' she said enthusiastically. 'But, personally, I like the Glaoui.'

She went over and knelt beside the carpet, examining it carefully. Khalil joined her.

'They come from my home area,' he said.

'The soft vegetable dyes are lovely,' she said, looking up at him. He seemed flattered that she liked them.

'Yes. And here you see the Glaoui style, which is their trademark,' he continued. 'Three styles of treatment. The carpet is knotted here, and here it is embroidered . . . and here it is woven.'

'Expensive?' she asked with a frown, calculating the likely cost.

'It's too early to talk prices,' he said. 'This is a co-operative, like most carpet warehouses. The night is young. We'll wander around a few places and then come back tomorrow, and then come back again and then we'll talk prices after a few glasses of mint tea. For the moment, let them show you some more. You mustn't expect to make any decisions straight away. Business is done at a slow pace here. It's a pleasure, not a chore. Enjoy the colours.'

She did. Sipping tea and watching endless carpets unfolded before her eyes, it was a very pleasant and leisurely way to spend an evening, particularly as Khalil began to unwind and became less difficult as time wore on. They wandered to two more warehouses and she began to differentiate between the carpets, even between areas in the High Atlas where some of them were produced.

'I think this has been a really good initiation into the carpet world, thank you,' said Hannah, genuinely grateful to Khalil. He was proving to be immensely valuable to her.

'I've enjoyed it.' He smiled. 'And I think everyone else did, too. You have quite a capacity for joy, Hannah.'

Hazily, taken aback by the compliment, she met his warm eyes. 'I feel very happy, right at this moment,' she said. 'Everyone's been very welcoming. Really friendly. I like the people of Marrakesh.'

'Good. You'll be involved with them a lot in the future, won't you?'

'I suppose so,' she said slowly. She hadn't really thought about future visits.

Khalil glanced casually at his watch and suggested they had something to eat.

'No, thank you,' she said cheerfully. She'd promised herself it would be business only. 'I'm eating at home tonight. Alone.'

'Wary of me, Hannah?' He grinned.

'Of course not, I'm not in the least bit bothered by you.' She laughed, as if the idea were ridiculous.

'Then you won't object if I treat you to a typical Moroccan dinner,' he said logically. 'With a bit of authentic music, and some entertainment thrown in.'

She was tempted, and said so candidly.

'Well,' he smiled, 'you wouldn't be able to walk into this place on your own, so you might as well make use of me.'

'Since you put it like that,' she said happily, 'I agree.'

It would be an idea to cement the new-found pleasantness between them. Let him treat her to a meal! Besides, she felt far too 'zingy' to go back to her little house now.

He ambled slowly through the market, past the insistent tapping coming from the jewellers' booths, past sacks exuding the fierce aroma of spices, and beneath the windows of a steam bath and the smell of sweet incense escaping into the chill night air.

Khalil retrieved Hannah from gazing open-mouthed at a street of cut-throat barbers doing a roaring trade in shaving heads, and finally stopped outside a low cedar-wood gate, set in a scruffy-looking high ochre wall, its knocker fashioned into the lucky Hand of Fatima.

Inside the gate there was a man on guard in an immaculate white silk tunic, short cape and knee-length trousers. Slung across his chest hung a crimson woven cord, matching his wide sash, and on the end of this cord hung a long curved dagger in a silver sheath. He bowed to Khalil and herself but she hardly noticed because she had been instantly entranced by the lovely floodlit gardens.

'Khalil! What a magical place! It's such a surprise! It looked so shabby from the outside!' she cried, her blue eyes dancing with delight.

'Ah. We keep our treasures hidden,' he said smoothly, waiting patiently as she surveyed the cool green and white tiled pool in the centre with its tinkling fountain. 'Berbers are nervous of showing their wealth. They prefer to keep it behind locked doors and thus cheat the Evil Eye.'

'It's very lovely,' she breathed, her lips parted.

'Almost . . . irresistible,' agreed Khalil huskily.

A quiver of awareness ran through her. She dared not look at him, though she knew very well that he was fixing her with those molten eyes of his.

'Yes,' she agreed, over-bright. 'And I think I'd like to make one or two changes to the decoration of our place in England. Can I get tiles like that, in those soft blues and greens?'

'I can get them for you, yes,' he said slowly, as if dragging his mind from thinking of something else.

She wandered around beneath the whispering mimosa. 'Tell me about those columns—and the carving—is that plaster? It looks like lace, it's so fine.'

'It is. A little like Granada, in Spain, isn't it? That's because once our Sultan ruled over North Africa and a large part of Spain, so the influence of Andalusian Moorish culture is very strong. The carving took twenty-five years to complete,' he said, sounding pleased. 'It was fashioned only with a hammer and a nail and its progress was measured in inches per day. A work of love and pride,' he finished softly.

'You Moroccans must have a great deal of patience,' she said in awe.

'We do,' he said, with a small smile. 'We certainly do. We will wait for a long time to get what we want. Come inside and have a look at the cedarwood ceiling. It's carved and painted. I think you'll like that, too.'

Khalil took her elbow and escorted her into a large, airy room. She gazed up at the wooden ceiling and its impossibly complex design. The room was very opulent. Thick red traditional carpets covered the marble floor and the tiled walls appeared to be gilded, rich golds on navy and sky-blue. A number of tracery arches led from the room, offering glimpses of other ornate rooms beyond.

'Here you can see the four elements of Moroccan art: wood, plaster, ceramic and marble,' he said, amused at her wide-eyed admiration. 'We paid the Italians a pound of sugar for a pound of marble.'

'You got the best deal,' she laughed. 'Where is the sugar now, after all?'

To the sound of the bubbling fountain just outside, she sat on one of the low brocade ottomans, scattered around the room haphazardly together with circular brass tables.

The staff were a bit slow to appear—more evidence of unhurried Moroccan life! Any minute, she expected to be handed a menu. She decided that this was presumably some kind of ante-room, since no other diners could be seen.

'Where do we eat?' she asked Khalil.

A man in a honey-coloured robe came through one of the archways just as she spoke, and bowed to them both, offering the traditional greeting.

'Wherever you like, Hannah,' he said softly. 'Outside in the garden, beneath the sky stitched with stars, or——'

She interrupted him, her senses alerted by the velvet tones of his voice. 'To hell with your embroidery. This is a restaurant, isn't it?' she asked warily.

'No, it's my house. I'm glad you like it,' he said lazily.

To Hannah, he sounded like a wolf about to devour a fat lamb. And it was she who was up for slaughter. How stupid of her to walk into his lair. She stared back at his sensual mouth, nerves rendering her speechless for several seconds.

'Why bring me here?' she managed, after a long, hot silence.

'To seduce you, of course,' he drawled.

CHAPTER FIVE

HANNAH stood up, disguising her trembling legs, and heaved an exaggerated sigh of exasperation. 'You said we'd eat Moroccan,' she accused sharply. 'With entertainment.'

'And so we will,' he murmured, detaining her by catching her hand. She gazed down stupidly as his long fingers curled around hers and the heat of their palms mingled. 'I think we can manage to make our own entertainment, don't you?'

Her mouth fell open. 'You rat!' she said in astonishment.

'Isn't that how you run your life, Hannah?' he asked, his eyes glittering. 'Exchanging favours? I'm only living by your creed, and by your morals. I introduce you to Marrakesh, you take me on a tour of the delectable Hannah Jordan.'

She almost admired his nerve. Her own sense of wry amusement kept her temper from rising. The system of barter in Morocco was even more highly developed than she thought! A grin spread over her face and she was aware that Khalil's eyes narrowed. He was puzzled—fine. She'd stay unperturbed and baffle him. That would keep her a few steps ahead of the devious lecher!

'No, it's not how I run my life,' she said calmly. 'As someone said earlier, we're not on a guided tour. Full marks for trying, but you really can't imagine I'll sink into your arms in gratitude because you took me to look at some carpets? You don't usually expect that kind of exchange of favours from women, do you?'

He fixed her with his ocean-deep brown eyes and she felt a treacherous quiver stab repeatedly within her body.

'I never speak of past conquests when contemplating a current one,' he said, his salacious glance devouring her body. Suddenly she felt cheapened by his insulting opinion, and the smile left her face. 'I thought we'd finish off the evening in beautiful surroundings, with a good meal, and end with the greatest pleasure of all,' he said huskily. 'One you enjoy, and I certainly do. I see nothing startling about that.'

Hannah was used to propositions. Normally she brushed them aside and felt no offence. Yet, surprisingly, it hurt her that Khalil should think that she regarded sex as a casual occupation to be indulged in whenever she felt like it. She should have remembered that he believed the exaggerated stories about Dermot's parties and her supposed reputation. A sour taste welled up into her mouth. Khalil was treating her like a whore.

'No, thank you,' she said sweetly, resisting the urge to flounce out in anger and go home. He'd know she cared about his opinion, if she did that. 'If you want to give me a meal, then fine; you'll be rewarded by my scintillating company, and perhaps a few arguments since we can never remain civil for long. If you want more return for your outlay, then you're out of luck. I suggest you send me home now and start searching for a woman who's prepared to swoon at your heaving manly bosom.'

He laughed, and his eyes crinkled so appealingly that Hannah found it hard to maintain her air of disinterest and cynicism.

'Very well. I see it's not the right time—yet . . . I'll settle for your company, a little sparkling conversation, a little quarrelling,' he agreed with a broad grin. 'That will be entertainment enough. For tonight.'

And he made no more demands. Later, when she curled up in her own bed—alone—Hannah wondered in amazement at how well the evening had gone. It shouldn't have done, considering that awful beginning, but after an uncomfortable few minutes they'd both stopped fencing and done justice to the meal.

It had been pleasant and—of course—unhurried. The warm, perfumed air had lulled their senses. The slow process of eating Marrakesh-style had meant that they had to fall back on conversation, and gradually the temporary 'cease-fire' had turned into a genuine absence of hostility.

Dinner had been traditional and superb, and surrounded with small courteous ceremonies. Her mouth drooled even now, remembering the flaky spiced pastry, frosted with sugar and cinnamon. And the pigeon pie...! She'd be vast if she kept eating so well.

Avoiding any topics which might raise bitter memories, she and Khalil had discussed the purchase of carpets and had made plans to visit the Atlas Mountains and see one of the country markets there, where she might pick up some cheap samples. They had pored over the map together and she had become very excited as he described the beauty of the area they were to visit.

They'd laughed a lot, bandied words, and Hannah had felt oddly exhilarated by Khalil's enthusiasm. His eyes had lost their wary chill and the sultry passion, and they had flickered with a thousand lights.

Always open to the delights of the world, she had found it easy to adore Marrakesh and the friendly people she'd met. And she had to admit that she was finding it difficult not to like Khalil, despite everything that had happened. Was this part of his determined seduction? If so, it was beginning to work, she thought ruefully!

Sighing, she rolled over in bed and reminded herself sternly of his bitter, vengeful behaviour. Beneath the charm, he still held a grudge against her, and he still regarded her as cheap—and fair game.

*   *   *

The morning bird-song deafened her. Fluting larks seemed determined to break the sound barrier with their din, and she struggled from sleep just after dawn. Dressing hurriedly in the chill morning air, she decided to pay a visit to the old town before she met Khalil at the Café de France, for coffee.

The bus was packed with people and she squashed in between some very well-cushioned bodies, and then panicked, remembering that she hadn't changed her money. She was a disorganised fool! But when she offered English coins, and expressed her distress in sign language, the people around her all contributed towards the correct fare, pressing it into her hand with smiles. She was very touched with their generosity and tried in vain to imagine that happening on the London Underground.

Hannah bought some dirhams the moment she found a money-changer in the market-place, and set off into the narrow, dark alleyways which were already thronging with a moving mass of life. She paused beside a carpenter's shop, redolent with the smell of unseasoned wood. A table leg was being carved by a primitive bow lathe, held between the carpenter's feet.

Seeing that she'd stopped, a child tried to sell her a cone of freshly roasted chick-peas—and then she was surrounded by children, pestering her, chattering, pleading. Smiles, frowns and sharp words didn't stop them. They followed her, catching her arm, almost pushing her along, demanding money.

'You give. Pretty lady. We show you, be guide.'

'No,' she said firmly. 'Go away.'

'See *medressa*. See palace.'

'Go away!'

'I hunger,' said a child, rubbing his stomach pathetically. 'Twenty dirhams.'

'No dirhams,' she snapped.

'Look, buy,' cried a girl in a veil and *djellaba*, draping scarves all over Hannah's shoulders.

Hannah gathered them up and calmly let them fall, noting wryly that the young girl caught them before they reached the ground.

'See museum, very cheap...'

They seemed to have no comprehension of personal space, or that they were intruding on her privacy. It was no use walking quickly—they walked faster, blocking her way, and she became rather irritated. It occurred to her that this hadn't happened when Khalil was with her.

And she came across the shop where she'd wanted to buy one of those earthenware saucers of solid cochineal, and some solid blocks of musk and jasmine. She stopped and had to physically push her way through the eager hustlers. The situation got worse when she attempted to bargain with the stallholder. He tried to take her hand and flirt. She withered him with a look and stalked away.

Two powerfully built teenage boys joined the group, shouldering everyone aside, and enthusiastically offered to show her the market and all the tourist sights. She thought wryly that they might agree to show her the Eiffel Tower if she asked.

The young men stared at her with their dark, liquid eyes full of admiration and she wondered just how safe she was, deep in the market, with no Europeans in sight. Despite her sharp and cutting retorts—which lost their force when delivered to males who only spoke broken English—her heart began to thud when one of the young men gave her a particularly persuasive and winning smile.

'You beautiful lady,' he said softly, his voice and eyes caressing.

Unnerved, she suddenly saw that they seemed to be manoeuvring her towards a dead-end. The teenagers moved in intimate contact with her, so that she was suddenly hip to hip with them, and she felt the unsettling warmth of their bodies and the smell of musk. The children were jabbering ceaselessly in their clamouring voices, small brown hands outstretched.

With a sense of inner panic she turned abruptly, pushed her way through the pedestrians walking behind, and began to stride away briskly. The persistent voices followed her. She turned a corner and went slap into something furry and hard, hanging down from a canopy. Instantly she recoiled.

It was a dead fox.

Hannah screamed in horror and whirled, flying blindly into a sharp piece of rusty metal protruding from the stall. She felt the sting of blood on her cheek but ran and kept on running, dodging down a maze of alleyways until she suddenly came to a place she knew: Khalil's house.

In utter relief that she'd reached safety, half sobbing and panting with exertion, she banged on the knocker. The guard opened the door, recognised her and the state she was in, and escorted her quickly into the house, taking her further in than she'd been before until she was standing in a richly carpeted room with a gold tented ceiling.

After a moment Khalil came in, his hair appealingly tousled, and hastily belting up a white silk robe. It was obvious to her that he wore nothing beneath and she averted her eyes, wondering if she'd jumped from the frying pan into the fire.

'Hannah!' He strode towards her and turned her around. 'Whatever is the matter? What's happened? Not that Irishman? He hasn't——'

'No,' she said, shakily. 'He hasn't. I'm sorry. It's stupid. I feel such a fool, I'm sure they weren't meaning to intimidate me——'

'Sit down,' he said sympathetically, drawing her beside him on to a heavy satin couch, as large as a mattress.

'Mahmoud, *qahwa, minfadlik,*' he said to the guard. And then he turned to Hannah. 'Mahmoud will bring us some coffee and you can tell me what happened.'

'It wasn't anything, really,' she said, feeling silly.

'It was enough to make you run, and,' he added with a sudden frown, 'to hurt you.'

Her hand shot to her cheek and found blood there. 'I went into the *souk* and got pestered by children,' she said, dabbing at her face with her handkerchief. 'I didn't handle it very well, I know that. I felt intimidated by two young men who... well, I didn't know how safe I was.'

'I doubt they would have hurt you, though they probably hoped you'd be bowled over by their charm and good looks.' He smiled. 'I did warn you.'

'I'm decently dressed,' she said truculently. Really, these Moroccan men were so arrogant! If a woman couldn't walk around without being assaulted...

'Stop bristling, Hannah. You can't be blind to the fact that you are a very desirable woman. Every country has its rules, its codes of conduct. Would you go into some British pubs on your own?'

'That's different. That's at night,' she said crossly.

'Oh? The British are only aroused at night?' he mocked. 'Take care, Hannah, and you'll be safer than in England. Step outside the boundaries and you'll be propositioned.'

'It's confusing,' she said reluctantly. 'It's hard when different cultures collide. I suppose I might have given the wrong impression, though I don't know how. But I didn't even know how to deal with the children, either. I ought to learn enough Arabic to tell beggars to go away.'

'Hmm.' Khalil's eyes lingered on her. 'You shouldn't have gone in alone until I'd talked to you about hustlers and guides, or till everyone in there had seen us together a few times and knew you weren't to be bothered. They'll get used to you in time and leave you in peace.'

He waited till Mahmoud had deposited a silver tray with a long-spouted coffee-pot and tiny cups. She accepted a cup from the guard, who spoke anxiously to Khalil and nodded at his reply, giving her a sympathetic grin.

'Mahmoud says he's relieved that you're all right,' said Khalil, sipping the hot spicy coffee. 'He was very concerned that a guest in our city should have been in distress.'

'Did you tell him I'd been a fool?' she asked wryly, keeping the handkerchief against her cheek.

'Of course not. But you must understand that you're a legitimate source of income for those young lads.'

'They ought to be at school, not begging,' she commented sharply.

'School isn't compulsory. After a certain age it's expensive, anyway. I did the same as they, once, earning money by bombarding tourists with requests to be their guide. I don't like it, I dislike their loss of pride, but you can't blame them.'

'I feel an idiot.' She sighed.

'You had no idea it would be like that. Your knowledge of Morocco comes from reading, after all. I can't recall Dermot mentioning irritating hustlers in his books. He always made Marrakesh sound like paradise,' he said drily.

'It has its flaws, then, like everywhere else,' she said.

'And everyone else,' he answered with a meaningful look.

'Lovely room,' she said brightly, changing the subject. 'It looks like a harem.'

'It was.'

'Oh.' Disconcerted, Hannah looked to see if her cheek had stopped bleeding and found that it hadn't. Khalil turned her chin around so that he could see the wound, and she felt immediately unnerved by the spread of his broad half-naked chest, so close to hers. Her breathing became infuriatingly shallow.

Without comment, he rose and walked over to a low, painted table, bringing back a gold jug and basin which he proceeded to pour over her handkerchief. Gently he dabbed at her cheek, while she held her breath so that he wouldn't discover how ragged it would be. The water was soothing and slightly fragrant, rather like him, she thought hazily, wishing he didn't have such long, curling lashes. Animal magnetism oozed from every one of his pores, knotting her up inside.

'How did you do this?' he murmured softly, his breath soft on her face and making the downy hairs stand on end.

'I—I ran into a stall. It seemed to be selling dead foxes. We don't have much call for dead fox shops at home,' she joked shakily. 'I whizzed around and went straight into a rusty bit of iron.'

His face was wreathed in smiles and the flash of his white teeth made her edge away in dismay. Gently he drew her back again.

'You bumped into a herbalist's shop, selling herbs, potions and magic,' he said, stroking her face with maddening deliberation. 'It seems to have worked for me. My good fortune.'

'Magic?' she croaked.

'Spells. Love-potions, aphrodisiacs...' His voice trailed away.

Hannah swallowed hard. 'I'm...' She cleared her throat again. 'I'm surprised you admit to needing stimulation.'

His eyes laughed at her. 'I don't. Especially with you around. Other men and women aren't so lucky. Think yourself fortunate that you didn't tangle with anything more gruesome. They sell some remarkable items.'

'Hasn't it stopped bleeding yet?' she asked in a husky tone, unable to stand the gentle rhythm of his fingers on her face.

'Oh, yes, ages ago,' he said innocently. 'Hold still.'

'But why, if you've——' She met his eyes and her voice faded, lost somewhere in the sudden plummeting of her stomach and the lift of her heart. He was going to kiss her.

'Now, Khalil,' she said breathlessly as his head angled and his lashes lowered. 'That's unfair. I'm shaken up and you're taking advantage——'

'Oh, I always play dirty,' he murmured, covering her mouth with his.

The brief contact with his warm, silk-clad body was nectar, balm to her soul. Regretfully, and very slowly, Hannah pushed him away, blinking at him with troubled eyes. 'I don't want you to touch me,' she croaked.

'Liar,' he said calmly.

He gently stroked her hair and let his fingers drift to her shoulder. 'I'm quite enjoying your teasing,' he said softly. 'But I ought to warn you that I'm getting more famished with every morsel I'm offered. A light aperitif is all right, but it sure as hell makes me hunger for the main dish.'

Hannah had regained her senses. 'The main dish is off,' she said with a cool tilt of her head. 'And there's definitely no dessert.'

'You're an extraordinary woman, Hannah,' he said, his eyes inscrutable as he leaned back nonchalantly on the mattress, his beard dark against his tanned face.

His robe had fallen open to reveal his husky chest and one strong, muscular thigh. Hannah tore her eyes away from his body with difficulty, the old pain of desire searing through her veins. 'I know,' she said with a casual air, playing for time and composure.

'You're an eighteen-year-old girl: sweet, innocent, and on the threshold of your life,' he said relentlessly, as Hannah pretended to be more interested in pouring herself another coffee. She was wondering how she could extricate herself gracefully, and go. His tone sounded ominous. Too sexy by half. She hardly dared to listen. 'You're a cold, hard-hearted gold-digger who's sold her soul. You're a confident, friendly and beautiful woman, who sends out sensual messages. Which one is the real Hannah Jordan?'

'All of them,' she answered, slanting him a look over her coffee cup. 'And more. Don't categorise me, Khalil. I don't fit into anything you might label me with.'

'I wouldn't dream of it,' he said lazily, staring with carnal eyes at her legs.

She resisted the urge to cover them up hurriedly. Let him look.

Khalil's sultry dark eyes lifted slowly, to flash fire into hers. 'So sure of yourself, aren't you?' he breathed.

'Yes,' she lied, with a toss of her massed hair.

'The trouble is,' he said, standing up suddenly and determinedly removing her cup from her hand, 'I'm equally sure of myself. And sure of you, of what you want.'

She swallowed, and was dismayed to find that he'd seen her nerves and was smiling to himself, his damnably sensual mouth curving desirably.

'You know?' she said, casting around for help from any source, her voice infuriatingly breathy. She needed a good put-down. 'How clever and perceptive of you. You actually know that I want a plate of baked beans on toast?'

He laughed gently. Her eyes shut involuntarily, and she groaned, longing for him, incapable of allowing herself to be free and reach out for what she really wanted because he'd think so badly of her. Catch twenty-two.

'I know what you want,' he repeated huskily. 'Your defences are very good, but not good enough. Every time I come near you, your body sings, doesn't it? I know, because it calls to me. A siren song. Desire pours from you in hot shock-waves. That can't be faked. Nor your body language.'

His hands reached out and she took a step backwards, but he advanced rapidly with menacing determination and enclosed her in his embrace before she could escape.

'I'm beginning to think we were destined for each other, Hannah,' he said softly, his mouth unnervingly close. 'Maybe you are a woman of ill-repute, but you have the ability to arouse me more than any other woman I've ever known in the whole of my life.'

'You're reading the signs wrongly again,' she said in a harsh, unnatural rasp. His face looked heart-wrenchingly tender and it was taking all her will-power to lean away from him.

'I don't think so,' he murmured. 'I don't think so at all, otherwise your heart wouldn't be fluttering so wildly like a little frightened bird against my chest.'

'That's no little bird. That's fear,' she said with a gulp, as he pressed her closer to him and the soft cushion of her breasts flattened into the hard muscle wall of his body. 'I don't trust you to behave like an honourable gentleman and respect my wishes. I'm naturally a little unsure of your intentions.'

'Then let me make them clear,' he breathed.

She wanted him to do just that. Paralysed by her longing, she could make no protest; her defensive repartee was silenced. Khalil stared deep into her eyes, his mouth slightly parted.

They kissed. Long, endless, raiding kisses, which had her walking on air as the minutes lengthened and time itself seemed to stand still. And all the while she was losing ground with every accelerated beat of her heart and the flooding heat which sought to overwhelm her principles. Hannah groaned inwardly as his lips moved, plundering tenderly, sweetly, coaxing and persuading hers into a response. She knew her resolve was slowly being destroyed and her resistance shattered for ever.

'Hannah!' he muttered roughly. 'I want you!'

She sought for a lifeline, something to break the terrible chains which held them together. 'You have to let me go!' she cried, wrenching herself away.

Khalil's mouth paused in feathering her throat and swept upwards relentlessly, increasing its pressure. He kissed her lips savagely, till they felt bruised from the assault. She kept her muscles tensed, and eventually he drew back, his face heavy with desire.

'Surrender,' he breathed. 'Think what it'll be like, between us——'

'Never!'

He seemed to realise that she meant what she said with every bone in her body, for his grip on her tightened viciously. 'Why?' he snarled, his eyes black with threat.

'Because of Dermot,' she said wildly.

He froze. 'Meaning?' he asked.

Hannah moistened her nervous lips. He looked very menacing. But she was committed. For her own sake, she had to go through with it. And what she was about to say was truthful.

'You know what I felt about him,' she said tremulously. 'I don't think I'll ever get over losing him. No—no woman ever forgets the man she loved and lost.'

She tried to master her breathing and inject some kind of coldness into her eyes, as Khalil's mocking gaze scanned her white face. His expression was unreadable.

'Oh, I think we've made a promising start,' he said, letting her go with an insulting caress of her thigh.

Hannah blinked as she staggered back. That wasn't the reaction she'd expected. She'd failed to crush his ardour as she'd hoped, by reminding him of her relationship with his stepfather. Instead, he seemed prepared to abandon his seduction and try again another time.

It rather annoyed her that he was able to turn off his so-called passion for her so easily. He was almost indifferent. *Indifferent!* While she simmered!

Hannah gave a wry smile at her illogical irritation. She ought to be glad. He was obviously not that eager. It had been merely another casual encounter to him. There must be plenty of other fish in the sea. The hotels must be bursting with women who'd love to be seduced by him. Like that blonde he was going around with, taking to bed, pleasuring...

Jealousy seared through her, catching her unawares. Through her head whirled visions of Khalil, looking as he did now, tousle-haired, seductive, his mouth inviting a young blonde woman to enjoy him, to taste his body... An involuntary gasp from the sharp pain emerged from her lips.

'Something hurting you, Hannah?' asked Khalil innocently.

She found that she'd been standing stock-still like a fool and he'd been watching her with mocking eyes.

'Only my shoulders, from your brutal assault,' she said coldly. 'I'm going. I ... I have some letters to write and some business to catch up on. So I'd like to cancel our arrangements and stay at home.'

'Of course. I understand perfectly,' he purred. 'Mahmoud will drive you,' he added politely, seemingly not at all put out. 'I'll collect you at nine tomorrow and we'll begin bargaining for carpets in earnest. We'll spend a few days in the city making arrangements and then I'll take you further afield. All right?'

'Yes, fine.' She hesitated.

'Something else, Hannah?' he asked softly.

'No, goodbye,' she said in confusion.

He eyes laughed at her. 'For a mature, well-balanced woman, you certainly don't seem to know your mind, do you?' he taunted.

'Oh, I know my mind very well,' she defended irritably. 'And, what's more, I know yours. Stop seeing me as a sexual challenge, Khalil, and let's get on with the business in hand.'

He flicked her an amused look. 'We will make spectacular advances. My behaviour will be impeccable, Hannah,' he promised.

It was. And, because of that, she felt oddly disappointed and disturbed throughout the following few weeks. Every morning she woke to lyrical larks and the scent of orange-blossom. Then came the sound of soft Irish songs, as Patrick moved about his little house next door. Every morning she became more breathless as the time came for Khalil to pick her up; each day she spent a ridiculous amount of time getting ready. She knew what was happening, but couldn't stop it.

The clean, bright air invigorated her each time they drove towards the city, with its incomparable vista of the beautiful Koutoubia minaret, blue skies, palm trees and the snow-capped mountains beyond. Every moment in Khalil's company was enjoyable, every accidental touch a sweet pain.

He was so indifferent to her that she knew he must be satisfying himself elsewhere, because sometimes he was tired and said he'd slept hardly at all, his eyes dark smudges in his handsome face. The cruel knives of jealousy twisted inside her and made her edgy. On those days, Khalil was quiet, as if he had no energy for small talk, and Hannah had to force her mind not to think what he'd been doing the night before.

He introduced her to his city with love and affection for it, involving her in its warmth, friendliness and leisurely atmosphere. They drank coffee with his friends, ate kebabs from the cookshop, and soon she became familiar with Marrakesh and the Marrakshi. And Khalil.

He was unfailingly courteous, quite reserved, and a perfect gentleman. It was driving her mad. To keep her sanity she often lunched with Patrick, who filled her in on the blonde whom Khalil met often, swimming with her in the hotel pool and apparently unable to keep his hands off her.

'She was all over him, too,' said Patrick. 'Larking about they were, in the water, swimming underneath each other——'

'Patrick,' she said sharply. 'I don't think you ought to gossip like this.'

'Gossip?' he cried in astonishment. 'Sure, it's no gossip.'

She shut her mind to it. She knew what was happening to herself. Khalil was weaving a spell over her. He had aroused her, and left her unsatisfied. He had reawoken her love.

Apart from those fleeting moments when her hand brushed Khalil's or their shoulders bumped when they were jostled, there was no physical contact between them and certainly no hidden innuendo in anything Khalil said.

But, for her, the sexual tension between them deepened, nevertheless, till Hannah shortened their days together because she felt like groaning aloud sometimes at the intolerable pressure she was under.

He hardly noticed that sensuality poured from him, that she had to hide her reactions when his warm melting eyes lingered on her. Instead, he generously devoted a great deal of time to ensuring that she made some good bargains. Among the thousands of little shops in the *souk*, he had selected a few which she had established as her future suppliers. His office had been put at her disposal and she'd set up a telex information link with Frankie, and had been delighted that everything was so well advanced. She'd be able to leave Marrakesh earlier than planned.

That was the trouble. She didn't want to.

CHAPTER SIX

ONE particular day worried her more than previous ones. They'd arranged to drive into the mountains. It would be an all-day trip, when she'd be constantly in his company. Give her strength!

Hoping to feel dazzling, she put on her brightest red dress and tied ribbons in her hair to cheer herself up. It didn't work. She couldn't sparkle.

'You're unusually quiet this morning,' he commented.

They'd driven out of the city on the Ourazazate road, far into the palm groves, without exchanging a word.

'I had a heavy night,' she said, glumly staring at the rampant prickly pears. She felt as prickly as them, that morning. She no longer slept like a baby. Sleep eluded her.

'Didn't we all,' he drawled.

She stiffened, fighting back a wave of misery and anger. 'I'm tired, Khalil,' she snapped. 'Don't make clever remarks.'

He took one look at her pale, drawn face, slowed the car and parked on the edge of the road. Hannah glowered at the long, straight avenue of eucalyptus trees ahead. The plain of Marrakesh stretched out for miles, flat and green, fed by the melt-waters of the Atlas Mountains. Given life and fertility by them.

Khalil had the potential to give her life, she mused. But, because he thought she was worthless, he wasn't bothering to divert his course for her. He flowed on, relentlessly, where he pleased, leaving her dry and dull. And parched.

'I don't know what you've been up to, these last few weeks, but it's not doing you much good,' he murmured. 'Do we have Patrick to thank for your lethargy?'

'Once and for all, Khalil,' she grated, 'Patrick is not my lover. I don't have a lover. I'm here to work.'

'No lover. I wonder why you're so tired and irritable?' he mused. 'Do you want to cancel the trip today? To go back and sleep it off?'

The idea of being alone with her thoughts disturbed her. That was bad enough at night, trying to work out why she was falling for this renegade. 'No. I want to wind up my business in Morocco as soon as possible,' she said tightly. 'And get back to London. And Frankie,' she added, thinking wistfully of her friend, who would soon help to talk her out of this mad, crazy infatuation.

'Frankie? Why?' he demanded, frowning.

'Because she...' Hannah bit her lip in annoyance. 'She.'

He shifted slightly in his seat. Her eyes locked unwillingly on to his muscular thigh, draped with the fine Italian cloth of a particularly elegant pair of grey trousers. He looked especially devastating that morning, in a soft white shirt, open at the throat, and a black cashmere sweater which she longed to stroke. Nervously, she ran her tongue around her lips.

'I see. You want to go on. As you wish,' he murmured, starting the car. 'You're finding this a painful separation?'

'I miss home,' she said shortly, not liking his enigmatic expression.

Funny, she'd said that before she'd thought about it. She hadn't missed home at all. Hannah wanted to make conversation to prevent herself from thinking why that should be. 'Mind you, I like Marrakesh. This scenery is lovely,' she gabbled on frantically, trying to be scintillating. 'Biblical herds of goats, a sea of palms and an icing-sugar wall of mountains.'

He smiled at her, his lashes fringing his eyes enticingly. Hannah felt desperate. They hadn't even spent an hour together and she was yearning for him.

'Your metaphors are a bit mixed,' he said drily.

Hannah turned to him in genuine surprise. 'Khalil, you amaze me,' she said. 'Where *did* you learn your English? Not purely in school, surely?'

It was a moment before he answered. 'Dermot taught me,' he said in a low tone.

'Dermot? Oh, Khalil, will you tell me how he met you?' she pleaded fervently. 'I hate mysteries.'

'Perhaps I should. You're less of a stranger now than you were. There's a bond growing between us, isn't there?'

'Huh!' she scorned.

Khalil threw her a brilliant smile. 'Well, Dermot appeared late one evening when I was six or seven and quite a rebel, evading school, working the tourist trade by playing on their sympathy,' he said, his profile softening with memories. 'It was the Night of Destiny. Fate.'

'I don't understand.'

'Late in the month of Ramadan is the Night of Destiny, when the fates of men and women for the coming year are sealed. Mother was very superstitious about Dermot's arrival that night. He'd come to do an article on the Berbers—he was a hack journalist in those days. His car had broken down. I was coming back from some mischief and I led him to our house, eager for a reward.'

'How did you talk to each other, if——'

'We all spoke French. He accepted our hospitality for that night and spent ages talking to us—my brothers, sisters, and . . . and my mother. It was then that he must have had the idea of writing a book based on our lives.'

'You mean, *Berber Wife*?' cried Hannah.

Her mind was reeling from his revelation. So she did know about Khalil's mother, after all. She must be Nerma, the fiercely proud woman in Dermot's best-selling novel. The woman who single-handedly brought up her reckless, proud sons and sensual daughters. The woman Dermot had called for, when he died.

'He was charming, as the Irish can be,' said Khalil wryly. 'To us he was also rich. He would go to any lengths, Hannah, for his art—even marriage. At least my mother adored him. They spent hours talking. We told him everything about ourselves. We introduced him to our friends, our culture, our way of life. The day he finished the book, he packed everything he owned and left.' His mouth twisted into a cynical smile. 'He wrote many books from those two years he spent with us.'

'Are you telling me that he went through all that just to acquire an authentic story?' asked Hannah, distressed.

'I am. He never returned,' answered Khalil. 'We had no contact with him, and it was years before his conscience pricked him and he sent us money. He and mother began to correspond again, and she forgave him. He was a very winning man. Irish charm, again.'

Hannah was silent. She believed Khalil. Dermot was capable of such a thing. Yet it was a wonderful book. Then she frowned. He couldn't be telling the truth.

Khalil slowed the car to pass a group of laughing children carrying bundles of walnut bark, destined to be cut up and sold to clean teeth. Absently, he smiled at them and waved.

'Why did you come to see him?' persisted Hannah.

'You must understand that I didn't hate him at all. None of us did. He'd taught us English, and started me on my career, giving us an opportunity to lift ourselves from poverty. I'd flown to Ireland as part of a European tour to promote Morocco. I had some holiday owing to me and decided to see Dermot. Mother had died and there were a few things she'd wanted Dermot to have. It seemed courteous to visit him and spend a short time with him.'

'You were very tolerant with him. But not with me,' she said resentfully.

'It's easy to be tolerant with people who don't mean much emotionally. I'd fallen in love with you,' he rasped.

'We both acted foolishly.' Hannah's heart was skipping beats.

'Yes,' he growled. 'I was particularly stupid. But not any longer, Hannah,' he said menacingly. 'This time I know my way around.'

'You mean you're a geography graduate, as well as a linguist?' she asked with cool innocence.

He chuckled, his eyes warm upon her, lighting her up inside. 'You're a good fighter, I'll say that.' For a moment he was quiet, negotiating a path between dozens of donkeys and their owners, who had sprung up as if from nowhere. 'Fortunately for you, we've reached the turning to the Berber market,' he said.

'Is this where we might pick up some rugs?' she asked, glad to avoid a personal discussion.

'That and to do a little general shopping,' he said, slowing down to accommodate the large number of donkeys and carts on the mud track.

'It looks pretty popular,' she commented.

'It's been held every week, exactly the same, for centuries. Nothing changes much out here. Berbers run their own lives. They tend to disregard authority.'

She fell silent, thinking of the vast differences between their two cultures. The Berber people sounded pretty lawless.

The market consisted of little more than a vast number of people, gathered together in almost medieval chaos. To Hannah, it felt as if she were transported to another era, a far more primitive way of life than one she'd ever seen before.

Each family, or each person, had brought surplus food to sell and barter. Some sat behind a small pile of produce, others lorded it over a cornucopia of riches from the earth.

The donkeys appeared to be making for a walled enclosure, guarded at its entrance by a man taking money. When they reached it and she peered inside, she saw that it was a huge donkey park, with the donkeys wandering around untethered.

'When I was a guide, I used to tell the tourists that this was the equivalent of a Sainsbury's car park. And that's the local Wimpy,' grinned Khalil, pointing to a line of men standing behind makeshift tables.

'Cheaper overheads, I see.' Hannah smiled, eyeing the few pieces of firewood and the oil drum making up the fire. A huge kettle steamed away on top, and one of the men was skilfully skinning tomatoes over it. He passed her one to eat and they stayed for a few moments, watching the men chop onions with all the skill of a West End chef.

'I find it hard not to break into my guide's patter,' murmured Khalil.

'Don't hold back on my account,' she urged, trying to take everything in. 'I'm fascinated. I don't like the poverty, though. It's odd, because the vegetables and fruit are out of this world. Are they very cheap to buy? Is that why everyone is so poor?'

'You mustn't mistake humble clothes for poverty,' admonished Khalil, leading her through the pathways between the scores of men sitting in front of high-quality produce. He bargained and bought a bag of walnuts, some figs and a bolt of white silk.

'But look there... That man only has a few herbs to sell.'

'Maybe he's here for the fun of it. Maybe he has business: herds to sell, horses for stud. Everything is not always what it seems on the surface, Hannah.'

'No. I know that,' she said in a low voice.

He looked at her out of the corner of his eyes. 'Then you are indeed learning. Don't worry about the prosperity of the people. Later you'll see rough mud buildings. Inside, they're like palaces. If you could see the women's jewellery you'd know it is priceless.'

'But that's inherited, surely?' she suggested.

'Yes, and some is modern, from their new-found wealth. The government protects the Berbers because agriculture is so important. They enjoy interest-free credit and no tax. Look around you. See how healthy everyone is.'

'You own land, don't you?' she asked, waiting while he bought a huge bag of mint.

'I do. After we've seen the mountains, I'll show you.'

'No, thank you,' she said hastily. 'I'm not in a hurry to end up in one of your harems again.'

'Nevertheless, I wish us to visit. My family are there,' he said curtly. 'They know I'm in this area. It would be unforgivable if I didn't call in.'

Hannah was annoyed with him. He hadn't mentioned this before. Yet part of her was curious to know what his country home and his family were like. She gave an inward sigh, wondering whether she was a fool to be getting deeper and deeper into his life.

He sent her to examine the carpets and try her hand at bartering alone for the first time. Her attempts at making herself understood were hampered by the sound of copper-beaters on the stall next door, but eventually she struck a bargain and returned to him, triumphant, with an armful of cheerful peasant rugs, adorned with animal motifs.

'Not bad,' he conceded, when she told him what she'd paid. 'Did you realise these were pure Berber? No other Muslim would reproduce the form of animals or people. The Koran forbids it, but the Berbers run their own version of the religion.'

'They sound like a very independent people.' She smiled. 'I did wonder why the man didn't understand my Arabic greeting, though.'

'The language is quite different. It isn't written, for a start. And it's much older than Arabic. The overworked letter-writer over there has to be a skilled linguist, translating Berber into Arabic or French. Seen enough?'

They left the market and continued along the road, climbing steadily through beautiful green hills and valleys, the foothills of the Atlas. Then the road climbed. It became narrower and full of hairpin bends, and she shifted closer to Khalil nervously.

'I don't like heights much,' she muttered.

'Oh, shame. How very unfortunate. Hang on to me,' he said softly, driving a little faster.

She clung to his warm shoulder, glancing down helplessly at the steep ravines. The road grew slippery with ice, and snow appeared in shaded hollows in the rock. Above them, vultures and kites circled in the hard blue sky.

'This road must have taken years to build,' she said. 'I suppose it was a caravan route?'

'This isn't the original pass. The old route passed through Telouet, where my mother's rapacious ancestor Hammou Glaoui had his stamping ground. He held sway over vast salt deposits. Caravans wound their way to his stronghold from the four corners of Africa. This road was built by the French purely to avoid his punitive demands.'

'Miles of tarmac road, just to avoid one man?' she cried in amazement.

'A dominant man,' he said, looking down on her with slow-burning eyes. 'A leader. One to be feared. He had the power of life and death over thousands.'

She gulped, imagining what Khalil would have been if he'd lived in those days. She doubted that he would have had any qualms about seizing her and forcing her to become his concubine.

'Sounds like a nasty piece of work,' she said tartly.

'I think he was. But that's judging him by our standards today. In those days it was normal to behave as he did, and people would have thought him weak if he did otherwise. Especially the women, of course.'

'I'm glad I'm not living in those days. I'd hate to be treated as if my feelings didn't matter.'

'You like your men to satisfy *you* first?' he murmured.

'You know what I meant.' She frowned. 'Why do you have to turn everything into a sexual innuendo?'

'I think it's something to do with the curve of your waist, the swell of your hip, the——'

Hannah tensed suddenly as the car began to slide, and she yelled in terror. *'Khalil!'*

They skidded. Hannah buried her head in his shoulder and he steered the car expertly, bringing it on course again. She lay against him, cradled by his arm, trembling.

'We had plenty of road. There was no danger. I'm an old hand at this. All under control,' he said huskily.

'I'm not,' she mumbled, sitting back in her seat.

'Neither am I, actually,' he breathed.

He caught hold of her hand which lay on his chest and lifted it to his mouth, kissing each finger passionately, while Hannah sat paralysed at the wantonness of her desire. She had no idea what she was more frightened of: the sheer drop to one side, possible oncoming traffic in the middle of the road, or the pleasurable sensation of Khalil's lips.

'How much longer?' she asked in a harsh, rasping voice and snatching away her hand, unable to bear his erotic mouth nibbling her fingertips any longer.

'Oh, nearly there, Hannah,' he said earthily. 'Don't you think?'

'I meant the end to this road,' she snapped.

'So did I.' He grinned. 'We're almost at the pass. The road is fairly straight for a while. Isn't it wonderful?'

She flicked a worried glance at the snow-covered mountain as he careered around the hairpin bends.

'It's frightening. I've never been able to cope with heights.'

With a gentle smile, he pulled her to him and she didn't resist. Cradled against his body, she felt more afraid of her own feelings than the dangerous bends and the ravines. But she needed to be close to him. He comforted her.

'It is frightening,' he answered in a whisper. 'But exciting, too.'

The car rolled to a halt and Hannah took a nervous look out. But Khalil wasn't interested in that. He caught her chin between his finger and thumb and turned her face to his.

'Very exciting,' he muttered.

'No!'

In alarm, Hannah pushed at his chest and, without thinking what she was doing, opened the car door and jumped out. All she wanted was to escape, and it was a few seconds before she realised that she was trying to run in deep snow. Shivering, she plunged into a drift and fell flat on her face, coming up floundering, bitterly cold, and furious.

'I hate you, Khalil ben Hrima!' she raged. 'I hate the way you try to inflict yourself on me whenever possible!

I hate your touch. It makes me cringe! Leave me alone! You're an arrogant, self-opinionated rat!'

He stood almost knee-deep in the snow, laughing at her cynically as if he didn't believe a word. Something within Hannah snapped and she stumbled through the snow towards him. He bent and moulded a handful of snow, aiming it at her and hitting her full in the face. She gasped in outrage and set her mouth in a grim line, every inch of her body quivering with rage. In retaliation she flung a huge snowball at him, which he ducked effortlessly, then they were pelting each other like frenzied children and suddenly she found herself laughing with exhilaration, echoing his roars of laughter.

In an unguarded moment they were in each other's arms, embracing and kissing, their faces glowing with the cold and exertion, their bodies pressed hard together as if they never wanted to be separated. Hannah felt his fingers gently massaging her scalp and the wonderful sensation of surrender to the moment. It would be over soon, regretfully, and she didn't want it to stop yet.

But his tender lips lifted from hers and he pushed her away, running a shaking hand through his tousled hair.

'We're running the risk of turning into snowmen.' He laughed unevenly.

In the clean, rarefied mountain air, Hannah thought he looked like a god of the High Atlas. She chided herself for her romantic sentimentality. It wasn't like her at all. Inside it seemed that her body had turned to molten liquid and her mind had slowed to a pure treacle sludge. He was turning *her* into a moron. Love was killing her brain cells, one by one.

'Something has to freeze your ardour,' she said ruefully.

'Someone has to heat up yours. Come back to the car.'

He helped her in and rubbed her arms till they were warmer. Then he removed his own jumper and slid it over her head, kissing her forehead as it appeared, then her nose, and then her lips.

'Khalil——'

'I'll turn the heater on full,' he said thickly, drawing the sweater over her unresisting body. His hands moulded it to her breasts and her eyes closed in ecstasy. 'Warming up?' he asked.

She nodded, not trusting herself to speak. She felt his fingers lightly stroking her face and his lips gently nibbling her earlobe. It made her quiver. Her eyes opened, drowsily.

'This is dangerous,' she began.

'Terribly,' he agreed, his long black lashes fluttering on his cheeks as he touched his mouth to her jawline.

A deep shudder ran through her and he drew back with a reluctant sigh. 'I think hot soup, a change of clothes and a warm welcome are needed to stop you catching a cold. We'll take the road to my home. I can't wait for you to meet my family,' he said soberly.

Hannah dropped her eyes. 'I wonder if that's wise?' she asked, frantically trying to understand him. Why bring a good-time girl into the heart of his family?

He gave a mirthless laugh. 'We gave up wisdom a while back.'

She let out a long sigh. 'You can say that again.'

'Well? You know I want to visit them.'

Hannah saw the raw longing in his face. From Dermot's book, she knew the devotion of Nerma's family to one another and could imagine how eager Khalil was to see his brothers and sisters. It was impossible to refuse him, the way he was looking at her.

'Why not?' she agreed. 'We have nothing to lose.'

'And everything to gain,' he said meaningfully.

Her face became anxious. He was up to something. 'This isn't another "come to the best restaurant in Morocco and see my etchings", is it?' she asked coldly. 'Because if it is, you're wasting your time. We fooled around in the snow back there and that's all it was. Don't read anything into it.'

'Now Hannah,' he said, sounding hurt. 'You don't take me for a fool, do you? I can differentiate between a game of boys and girls, and one of mothers and fathers.'

She didn't like to ask him what category their momentary lapse in the snow came into. Tense, and supremely aware of every inch of Khalil's virile body beside her, she reached into the back of the car for her shawl and huddled in it, sitting in morose silence as he drove up to the pass.

The road had recently been cleared and steam rose from it where the sun beat down. Khalil paused briefly so that she could take in the view and then, without a word, began the journey down the mountain.

'We're going on to the *piste*,' he said after a while. 'I warn you, it could be bumpy.'

Alarmed, she clutched at her shawl. 'My God! A *piste*? Isn't that a ski-run?' she gasped.

'No! It's a rough track. What we call our unpaved roads.' He smiled, turning off on to a narrow dirt path. 'You can see how it was impossible for even the Romans to subdue the people out here. For most of the year they were cut off, isolated by the snows. That's how they kept their own identity.'

'Dermot painted them as barbaric and lawless. Do you take after your mother or your father?' she asked.

She remembered how stubborn and powerful Nerma was in the book. She recalled the harsh life, the way she had bound her family together by the sheer force of her personality.

'You'd probably say I have the faults of both of them,' he said with a crooked grin. 'Too much arrogance, pride, a refusal to know when I'm beaten...a tendency to shock by unconventional behaviour...I had a very unusual upbringing, Hannah.'

'I know,' she said quietly.

His world was alien to her. They had nothing in common. How fortunate they'd never married. It would have been a disaster; she would never have adapted. The realisation made her feel very despondent. No wonder they argued. They saw the world from different points of view.

'Now I understand why Dermot fell hook, line and sinker for you,' he said huskily.

'What?'

'The similarity,' he said. 'Darken your hair, and you could be my mother's double. Strong, beautiful, with a ravishing personality. He was married to her. They did have some pleasure together. That's one of the reasons I——'

He stopped talking suddenly. Down the side of the mountain cascaded a red waterfall, dropping on to the road and tumbling down the precipice beyond.

'Hang on.'

'But you can't mean to cross!'

'I don't mean to go back.'

Hannah clutched at the dashboard, her heart in her mouth. Khalil drove straight through the gushing water. She subsided, shaking.

He patted her knee. That was almost worse.

'Relax. I have everything in hand.'

'My knee can come out of your hand, for a start,' she said sharply, removing his fingers.

He chuckled wickedly, a predatory note in his laugh. The scenery became greener as they descended, and the rivers more thickly laden with orange-red sediment. They reached a broad, boulder-strewn river-bed. It was impassable. Khalil came to a halt and got out of the car, surveying the scene. An entire section of the road had been washed away, and so had the bridge—a huge fifteen-foot section of it.

Khalil came to her side of the car and she looked up at him in dismay.

'I hadn't realised it was this bad,' he frowned.

'Can't we get over?' she asked, disappointed.

She'd wanted to see his home and meet his family, she realised. Heavens, she was stupid! She was willingly going to dig her own grave, it seemed, by linking herself more and more to him.

He gave her a long, calculating look and went back to scan the river.

'Let's give it a go,' he said blithely, getting into the car.

'Khalil, you don't have to prove you're macho. I swear, I believe it!'

'Have faith in me, sweet Hannah,' he murmured, leaning over and kissing her gently in encouragement.

As if he were driving down Park Lane, instead of a torrent bed, he casually put the car in gear. Hannah held on to his sleeve apprehensively as they bounced forwards.

'Don't worry,' he said. 'I wouldn't risk harming you.' He curved his hand around her knee and she jumped, so he slid his fingers further up her thigh. 'We have too much ahead of us, to take risks. I wouldn't want to miss the next few weeks, would you?'

'I want to miss the next few minutes. I want to go home,' she said anxiously, ignoring the raw ache in her loins.

'You are.'

'My home!' she exclaimed in panic.

'But Hannah, this will be your home.'

Khalil drove straight into the flood-water as she opened her mouth to protest. Hannah's attention was diverted and she gripped her seat in terror as the car surged through the orange river, which boiled angrily around the vehicle. Lurching over submerged boulders, and to the sound of scraping metal, she held her breath as Khalil struggled with the steering wheel, leaning forward, his face intent and his eyes glistening.

She shut her eyes.

'I'm going to try the brakes now,' came Khalil's voice.

Her lashes flickered open cautiously. They were safe! Looking back, she saw where they had come and shivered. He caressed her shoulder reassuringly.

'It's one hell of a road, isn't it?' He grinned.

'Don't do that to me again!' she cried fervently.

'Touch your thigh?' he murmured.

'Drive through rivers!' she yelled, infuriated.

'Ah. In that case, we'll have to stay at my house till the river goes down,' he said, sounding pleased.

'Oh? How long will that be?' she demanded.

'Could be months,' he replied, grinning.

'You devil! Don't make jokes! I can't stay, not even for the night!'

'Make your decision when you've met my brothers and sisters. You are welcome to stay, or return. I'll be sending men out to work on repairing the bridge.'

She subsided a little. His family would act as chaperons. 'You say it's your home, but your family lives there?'

'It's mine. There's always some of them there, visiting. We're coming up to a good view of it now.'

Placated, Hannah sat forward eagerly. They turned a bend and Khalil parked on a wide swing of the road. She was stunned by the breathtaking view.

Below them lay a lush green valley, which was dotted with olive trees and orange groves and the occasional dark column of a tall Italian cypress. The valley ran between low, crumpled hills, swathed in emerald-green rather like brightly rumpled blankets. Almost encircling these hills were the ever-present dazzling white mountains. But it was the centre of the rich pastures where the main focus of her eyes lay: a huge fortified castle—an enormous rambling kasbah.

'My house. The lands of the summer waters,' said Khalil in a voice of pride.

No wonder. This must be the most stunning setting in the whole of Morocco, she thought in awe.

'It's at quite an altitude,' he said, his eyes appearing to devour the landscape before him. 'Six thousand feet. You'd never know it, would you? But the mountains soar to over ten thousand feet here, and act as a barrier. One or two things are a struggle to grow, but we persevere.'

'I hadn't imagined anything like this,' said Hannah, still shaken by the rambling immensity of the building. She felt dwarfed by the vastness of his valley. Very insignificant. No wonder he regarded her as a woman to be coerced or bought. He must be used to buying whatever he wanted. 'A house in Marrakesh and this! You must be rich beyond most people's dreams,' she said slowly, trying hard not to be impressed.

'I have an apartment in Paris and Casa, and one in London, too,' he said. 'You like rich men, Hannah. You appreciate beauty. You won't find a more beautiful house than this.'

She felt nervous. He was definitely plotting something.

They passed a series of terraced fields, irrigated by gushing springs. By the frothing waters, women were washing clothes and laying them on rocks to dry; clothes of brilliant jewel colours.

'Berber women,' said Khalil, waving to them, his face alive with happiness.

Despite her apprehension, Hannah's heart lurched crazily. And then there was a sharp report and the car careered around the road, while Khalil fought to gain control and keep it off the jagged stones. They rolled to a halt with the front wheels driven into a bank.

'Puncture,' he frowned, going to investigate. 'Two punctures, curse it! Both front tyres. One of the hazards of living out here, I'm afraid.'

Hannah climbed out, dismayed. The wicked rocks had cut the tyres to ribbons. They were stranded in the middle of nowhere, and they hadn't passed another car for the whole length of the road!

'What are we going to do?' she asked anxiously. It looked like miles to his house.

'We'll make alternative arrangements,' he said complacently, beckoning to the women.

Hannah watched as they led their lone mule towards them.

'What do you think?' He grinned.

She looked uncertainly at the animal and then laughed ruefully. 'I suppose it's no use waiting for the next bus.' She sighed, letting the women heave her on. She giggled with them, enjoying their merriment.

'All aboard,' murmured Khalil, swinging up behind her.

'Oh, no,' she exclaimed, wriggling away from his warm body. 'We'll be too heavy together. You walk.'

'Like hell, I will!'

He clapped his heels against the mule's sides and they set off, to the laughter and barracking of the women.

Despite her misgivings, Hannah just found herself laughing, too, as they bounced along; laughing at their undignified progress and the uncomfortable jolting, but mainly in delight at being a real part of the landscape now. For somehow it was all different from the way it had been, from the inside of the car. The unpolluted air was clean and pure, and she could actually hear the bees humming and smell the strong-scented herbs, releasing their essential oils in the warm sunshine.

Khalil held her lightly but securely around the waist and, after some uncomfortable moments straining away from him, she leaned back and abandoned herself to enjoying the experience.

'Traditional buildings,' he said in her ear. 'Built in a square around a courtyard. Palaces inside. Remember?'

They were just above the mud-caked walls of quite a large farm, its terraced fields stretching down the valley. There were so many stones and boulders in the wheat-field nearest to her that she realised it could only have been sown by hand, and she marvelled at the patience needed. Khalil had told her that it was a Moroccan trait.

Peace surrounded them. Above, swallows rose high in the bright sapphire sky. The farmland gave way to fields of orange marigolds, planted beneath a cluster of almond trees in full blossom. Behind her, Khalil's body twisted and he suddenly presented her with a spray of wild yellow jasmine, its strong perfume quite overpowering.

She choked back her emotions. Khalil's hand ran along her arm and his mouth bent to kiss her neck.

'This is my real home,' he said, sounding emotional himself. 'Whatever I appear to be, whatever I wear, my roots are in this oasis, within the wild and untamed mountains. I knew you'd love it. I want you to find happiness here—I want you never to leave it. To stay always.'

'Stay? Always?' she repeated stupidly.

'Of course. That's why I brought you here.'

Hannah went cold. So that was what he was up to. He planned to put her behind locked doors. She stared in horror as the fortified stronghold loomed larger and larger, its magnificent lines now unnervingly forbidding. Out here, Khalil was asserting his dominance over her. She was being abducted.

CHAPTER SEVEN

'WHAT are you trying to do to me?' she asked in a choked voice.

His chuckle made a shiver run down her spine. She felt the slide of his hand, possessively rising to the curve of her breast.

'That must be obvious by now, Hannah,' he said throatily.

'Take your hand away,' she rasped. Hannah was terrified. All that talk about his family had been a ruse to get her here. He'd even boasted once before that he always 'played dirty'.

And now she knew a little more about his background, she could well believe it. Stubborn. Never admitting defeat. Unconventional... Oh, God! She knew enough about him to be aware that the shreds of civilisation would be stripped from him, now he was in this remote and barbaric world of his. There would be no one to call for help if he chose to force her to his will. This was his land. His people.

Yet, surprisingly, his hand dropped on to his thigh. Hannah swallowed, her throat dry with nerves, wondering if this was part of his slow torment.

'Don't be afraid,' he said. 'It won't be that much of an ordeal. It is my wish that my guests experience nothing but pleasure when they stay with me.'

Pleasure! Long nights of clever seduction? Unbearably slow torture as his hands, lips and eyes brought willing women to the brink of an erotic insanity? Hannah forced down her fears.

'How considerate,' she said sarcastically. 'If you think I'm going to enjoy what you have in mind, you're mistaken.'

Khalil dismounted and held out his arm to help her, his face puzzled. Hannah swung down on her own, and shrugged him off when he made to put his arm around her shoulder, staring at the fortress a little distance away.

'I'm sorry you're being so stand-offish,' he said quietly. 'I'd hoped you might want to please me in this matter.'

She whirled around, shaking with rage. 'Please you?' she spat. 'Please you? My God! You behave in the most despicable way possible, you spend weeks being charming and innocent, and then you spring this on me! Don't you realise I'd loathe every moment?'

'Hannah—I want you——'

'No! I won't! And if you try to force me, I'll resist with all my strength!'

He was deeply offended. His face had become devoid of warmth and only a distant chill lit his eyes. He slapped the mule's rump and it began to wander up the track where it had come from.

Hannah stood her ground defiantly. She might have insulted his male pride, but it looked as if his desire for her had vanished, and for that she was grateful. Even if she felt miserable. The gulf between them had become uncrossable, like the boulder-strewn torrent bed. Only someone as stubborn as Khalil would have tried to beat nature. And he hadn't given up on Hannah, despite all her protests. He'd take what he wanted. Forcing her at first, and then his lovemaking would be so infinitely desirable to her that she'd be a willing accomplice in her own downfall.

Khalil gestured towards the kasbah's massive iron-studded gates with a curt nod. 'We will have lunch,' he said icily.

'Prison rations?' she snapped.

He drew in a deep breath. 'Don't go too far with your insults, Hannah,' he growled. 'I only have a certain degree of control over my temper and you're dangerously pushing me to my limits. In!' He jerked his head again.

Knowing that she had no choice, she stalked to the gates with dignity and waited while he unlocked a small door set within them. Two servants came running across the inner courtyard, but he waved them away impatiently and the door clanged shut behind Hannah with a terrible air of finality, and she wondered if she should have been wiser to at least try to run away when she had had the chance, outside.

His hand clamped down over her arm, forcing her across the paved courtyard beneath the intimidatingly high walls. A green-tiled portico opened out on to a large room, though it was several moments before Hannah could see after the bright sunlight. But when she did she realised with dismay that Khalil was, indeed, a rich and powerful man, and he would expect to do as he liked with her.

For the traditional Moroccan decoration was more detailed, more ethereal than any she'd yet seen, the gold and silver leaf more refined, and the furnishings far more sumptuous. It must have cost a fortune to create out in the wilds, with Marrakesh so far away and no town of any size nearer than distant Ourazazate, the last trading post before the Sahara.

'Sit down,' he rapped.

'What a bully you are,' she seethed, refusing to obey. 'A real small-time tyrant, pushing a woman around. I imagine you've played this scene many times before. I doubt I'm the first woman you've dragged here and deprived of her virginity.'

'Virginity!' he yelled, beside himself with rage. 'You accuse *me* of immorality? You have the flagrant nerve to insinuate that I lure women here and treat them all like whores? You're the whore here, Hannah Jordan! How I even contemplated bringing you into my house, I don't know! I must have been crazy!'

Her eyes blazed. She threw back her head and lifted her ribcage, ready to give him a piece of her mind.

'Don't you dare flaunt yourself,' he snarled. 'Look at you! Proud of yourself! Presenting your body to me! Well, Hannah, perhaps you'll regret that. Perhaps you need teaching a lesson!'

Eyes glittering, he strode rapidly towards her. She backed away and fell against a silk mattress, with Khalil tumbling with her. The weight of his body imprisoned hers, his chest rising and falling in fury, crushing the breath from her. Terror clutched at her heart when she met the full savagery of his impassioned gaze. She'd pushed him too far.

The hard pressure of his muscular thighs bore down in ruthless, unnervingly masculine domination. Hannah knew she was helpless against him. A tremor ran through her. With one hand he held her jaw; the other caught hold of a handful of her hair and she found she couldn't move her head. His face was an inch or two away—thunderous, energised with wrath, his breath forcing hot and fast on to her lips. They tingled and parted. An electrical charge shot between them, making her gasp.

Before her eyes she saw the change in his face as an intense, powerful desire replaced the initial primitive rage. The carnal curve to his mouth made her tremble and her lashes fluttered at the repeated flurries of warmth coursing through her veins.

In the background, someone shuffled into the room as if they were wearing slippers. Khalil briefly turned and his ferocious expression must have deterred the intruder, since there was the sound of hastily retreating footsteps. Hannah groaned aloud. His authority was absolute.

'Yes,' he grated, his burning eyes boring into her head. 'Now it's only you and me. No one to interrupt us. And I can make you pay for your offensive words.'

'Willingly. I have two hundred dirhams in my purse,' she said with defiant composure.

Khalil's eyes narrowed in shock. 'You dare to joke? Curse you, Hannah! I curse myself for being so stupid. Once I actually wondered if you really were selfish and cheap, shallow and ill-mannered. Now I know you are. Every breath of your body, every word you utter, your entire behaviour has proved that.'

'I don't deserve your scorn,' she began.

'You deserve everything you're going to get,' he said menacingly. 'Every insult I can heap on you. Starting with this.'

His mouth ground into hers. Beneath his heavy, hard body, Hannah could barely move, though she tried. And then she became aware of the fact that her slight struggles were arousing him as the heat between them merged and shifted imperceptibly, her pelvis suddenly shockingly lodged against his, the subtle movement of her breasts rasping their hard peaks against his unresisting chest.

'Very good, Hannah,' he said hoarsely. 'Offer me more.'

'Please!' she gasped.

'Patience. Remember the exquisite delight of delaying fulfilment.'

'No, I——'

'Your eagerness not to delay is exciting me,' he whispered.

Khalil began to murmur his pleasure, increasing the delicious sensations their bodies were arousing by shifting his own weight rhythmically. His breathing increased its rate and his passion rose and the pagan light glittered in his eyes.

'*No, Khalil!*' she managed at last. 'Not like this——'

'Show me how, then,' he muttered against her mouth. 'Like this?'

Before she could say what she had intended, his tongue had slipped into her mouth's moist interior and a shudder of raw desire shook her whole being. Khalil's hands slid up the soft skin of her thigh, impatiently pushing aside the material of her dress. She went rigid, suffering the unloving kisses, the insolently roaming hands, tears welling in her eyes.

Oblivious to all but his own needs, Khalil deftly undid the buttons on her dress and her mouth was at last released as his head dipped to nuzzle her breasts. Hannah moaned.

'You animal!' she whispered.

'So. You like a man to be rough,' he said thickly. 'I give you what you ask for.'

She felt the sharp, greedy tug of his lips on her nipple and the answering beat of desire permeating her whole body. Wave after wave of wanton sensations threatened to starve her brain of sense. She writhed beneath him, perilously close to abandoning her principles.

'Kiss me, Hannah,' he muttered, lifting his head, his lips moist. 'Kiss me.'

The sound of his deep, impassioned voice echoed in her memory and for a moment they were the adoring young couple on that Irish hillside. She let out a low, defenceless groan and blindly reached for his head, pulling it fiercely to her mouth, arching her body with him as they rolled on the mattress. He raised himself slightly, pinning her arms above her head and looking savagely down on her face, which was flushed with desire, her hair tumbling in soft golden waves over the gleaming satin.

And then he stilled. He stood up swiftly and, when she lifted her trembling body to one elbow, she saw that he stood with his back to her as though trying to master himself.

'What am I doing? You bitch! You drag me down with you,' he whispered.

Hannah reeled with his words. From sheer habit, she sought sharp answers to that remark. Yet she kept her mouth shut for once. There was so much disgust in his voice that she dared not risk another assault with a defiant answer. He'd stopped. It was enough for the moment.

'Abdu!' he thundered.

Hannah jumped. A servant entered, perhaps the same man by the sound of his slippered feet.

'Sidi?' he asked, keeping his eyes resolutely on Khalil, whose rapidly panting breath sounded harsh to Hannah's ears.

What must Abdu think of her? Her hair falling in a dishevelled curtain, Hannah hid her head with shame, racked also with the evidence of Khalil's contempt for her. Now he must be convinced that she was a slut. Otherwise she wouldn't have behaved like that. What on earth had come over her? Her skin was tingling from her blushes and inside she felt sick with mortification.

'Miss Jordan is an English guest of ours. Bring something for her to eat and drink, please,' said Khalil tersely.

'English! I practise! Some *harira*? A little couscous——'

'No. Anything. Get something quickly. A snack.'

'And you, lord?'

'Nothing.'

'The children have food, by the river. You will eat with them?'

'Stop fussing, Abdu. I'll go and see them, of course. Where's everyone else?'

'Marrakesh, sir. They return tomorrow, *Insh'Allah*.'

'Tomorrow? Hell! How many cars have they taken?' frowned Khalil.

'All, lord.'

Cursing, Khalil gave instructions for his car to be repaired and then he threw a cold glance at Hannah.

'Abdu will bring you food.'

'I want nothing of yours,' she said proudly.

'Please yourself. I don't care what you do,' he snarled. 'Wait here till I come back. We'll settle our business once and for all.'

Panic made her jump up. 'Settle——!'

'Stay!' he ordered, in a voice which thundered across the room. 'Or, by the beard of Allah, I'll show you what my anger is really like! Make sure she doesn't leave,' he snapped at Abdu.

The servant looked uncomfortable and anxious, but nodded. Hannah was left alone in the room to ponder her fate. It didn't bear thinking about. Hesitantly she tiptoed to a filigree archway. No one stopped her. Emboldened, she walked quickly through and came out in the central garden, a peaceful area of bubbling fountains and green pools, of carefully tended orange trees and untamed cascading flowers.

It wasn't much use being in the middle of the fortified house. She needed to find her way back to the entrance—or find another exit. But that wasn't much use without transport. Maybe she could find those Berber women again, and hire a mule. Without a car himself, Khalil would find it difficult to follow her—unless he kept horses here, of course. She had a chance.

She heard a sound and her hand flew to her mouth, as Abdu came towards her bearing a tray which he set on a marble table.

'Lady, I bring a little salad, a little cold chicken. There is fruit and cheese.'

'Thank you,' she said faintly. Then she had an idea. She'd appeal to Abdu's male pride. 'Wait! Are you an honourable man, Abdu?' she asked.

'I am,' he answered proudly, drawing himself up.

'Then help me, Abdu,' she said with an impassioned cry. 'Khalil ben Hrima will hurt me. He—he will dishonour me. Help me to get out of here and back to Marrakesh——'

Abdu had taken a step backwards. 'Khalil is a good man!' he cried, shocked. 'He will not hurt you! You insult us all!'

Hannah looked at him in despair as he stalked off, tight-lipped. She'd have to find a way out on her own, then, and trust to luck after that. Picking up the glass of orange, she drank it all and pocketed some bread and fruit. It might be a long time before she had anything to eat again. Those villages beside the road were few and far between.

The garden was surrounded by arches and screens. She chose one and made for it, finding herself in a cool marble reception-room. Soon she had become immersed in a warren of rooms, all of which were lit by ornately iron-grilled windows. So vast was the building that Hannah became well and truly lost.

Several times she passed servants, who smiled and nodded at her in a friendly way but didn't attempt to stop her. After turning up in the garden for the third time, she decided to climb some stairs she'd seen and get her bearings from one of the upper rooms. If she could get to the flat roof, in fact, she might even discover another exit.

The roof was a long way above ground level and the view down made her feel giddy. What she did see was the breathtaking landscape, two storks' nests, and Khalil, a few hundred yards away, surrounded by laughing children. She glared, resenting the fact that his total lack of conscience allowed him to play games with the children while she waited, terrified, for him to appear and . . . A sob broke from her lips. Khalil was a callous swine.

Completely uninhibited by him, the little children were clambering all over him, tugging at his shirt and trousers to gain his attention. There was something painful to her in the way he adored them all and took evident pleasure in swinging them on to his shoulders, tickling them, tumbling them on to the ground.

Wrenching herself away from the scene, she plucked up all her courage and hung over the edge of the castellated parapet, peering nervously right down the walls, looking for an exit. Running frantically from one different level of the immense roof to another, Hannah finally realised the truth. There was only one way out: the front gate, and it was now guarded by four men with rifles.

Khalil would take with violence what she would once have given to him with love.

She leaned back against the parapet and tried to calm her hysteria. She was quick-witted and lively. She *must* be able to think of some way to get the better of Khalil.

'Hannah?'

She whirled, her trembling hands gripping on to the wall behind her as his dark head emerged from the stairway. She shrank back, glancing down at the drop, and shut her eyes as her stomach turned over.

'Don't come near me!' she gasped.

Two small figures came running up the steps. They wriggled past Khalil and ran towards her. The two young boys, dressed in rumpled robes, stopped at the expression of fear on her face, their brown eyes solemn.

'You insult my family and my hospitality, you insult my good name, but don't you dare refuse to greet my nephews,' said Khalil through clenched teeth.

She stared, uncomprehendingly.

'Good afternoon, Miss Jordan,' chorused the two boys in careful English. One of them realised how dishevelled he looked and attempted to straighten his robe and pull it neatly over the cotton trousers he wore beneath. Then he gave her a beaming smile.

Her tender heart went out to them. 'Good afternoon, gentlemen,' she managed.

There was a great deal of shouting from the stairs and Khalil was pushed up by a group of laughing children, all of whom greeted Hannah in the same impeccable English, with the same impeccable manners.

Khalil coldly introduced his nephews and nieces till her head reeled with their names. She noticed that, after she'd acknowledged each one, they returned to him, the younger ones fondly clinging on to a piece of his shirt, or fiddling with the plain gold watch and the rings on his hand. It appeared that he was a favourite, indulgent uncle. A man with two sides. Trust her to get the worst one.

He glanced down at the small children, patiently and quietly waiting around him. They met his eyes and beamed, one by one, as if he'd flicked on a switch. A pain sliced through her. She couldn't bear to look at his tender, loving face. Not when that love was denied to her.

She turned and stared blindly at the valley. A faint breeze ruffled her hair. A scent of herbs and spices drifted on the air, seducing her senses. It was so unfair. Even nature was conspiring against her, increasing the turmoil in her heart.

'Hannah?' Reluctantly she turned her head. He stood frowning at her, absently stroking the long black hair of a beautiful four-year-old girl. 'Are you admiring the storks' nests, or the view?' he asked after a long silence.

'Maybe I was thinking of jumping off,' she said evenly.

He said something to the children and, puzzled, they disappeared obediently.

'You wield a lot of power here, don't you?' she asked him.

'I rule over this area.'

'*Rule?* Good heavens, is this a tinpot dictatorship?' she scorned. But her fear had increased.

'Several villages and families have a special alliance. I happen to be the head of them. There are many such rulers. It's a loose kind of rule. We are all jealous of our liberty and guard it like a precious jewel.'

'Then you'll understand that I, too, want my liberty,' she said, tossing back her wind-blown hair.

'You will have it,' he answered harshly, 'once we have finished some unsettled business.'

'My God!' she breathed in horror. 'How can you be so clinical? I refuse to have anything to do with you. I won't make it easier for you by co-operating.'

'You must,' he snarled.

'Make me,' she challenged. 'See what little pleasure you get from victory.'

'You will put me in an impossible position!'

His eyes blazed at her, but she met them fearlessly. She refused to be intimidated.

'I'm sorry, Hannah,' he said, with a steely determination tightening his tone, 'but I can't accept your childish display of bad temper. I——'

'You *what*?' she gasped. 'You snake! You worm! You're the lowest of the low, Khalil ben Hrima!'

He went white around the lips. In a second he had covered the ground between them and was bending her back over the parapet. Hannah screamed and then, to her intense relief, he raised her, twisting so that she was flung against him like a rag doll, all the breath shaken from her body.

'I've taken all I can from you. You're a guest in my house! How dare you speak like that, you tawdry Jezebel?'

He hauled her to the top of the stairs, gripping her wrist. 'Either you come down with me peaceably, or I drag you down. Choose.'

'I can walk down on my own!' she yelled. 'You're hurting!'

'I have to get through your thick skull somehow,' he growled. 'Get down.'

Her wrist still clenched in his iron grip, she stumbled down the stairs and was pushed along a thickly carpeted corridor. Her heart flew into her mouth when he stopped at a heavy cedarwood door and kicked it open. It was, without any doubt, his bedroom.

'We won't be disturbed in here,' he grated.

The door was flung shut and she found herself pressed against it, pinned by the weight of Khalil's body, both wrists encircled by his bruising grip.

Her blue eyes flickered around the room nervously. It was in the colours of the desert, the walls lined with soft-hued sandy silk, the ceiling draped in a darker tone. Glaoui carpets covered the cedarwood floor and hung behind the bed. It was massive, in shades of tawny satin and draped overhead to form the shape of a Berber tent. Made for lovemaking, for stretching luxuriously, for... Hannah's eyes widened. For action.

Startled, her gaze returned to Khalil. He was staring at her with an extraordinary mixture of emotions on his face. 'Now tell me what you intend to do,' he muttered.

Her mouth dropped open. 'Do?' she repeated stupidly.

'About severing our business relationship.'

She raised her eyes to heaven. 'My God! Frankly, Khalil, I'd like to sever your head!'

'Maybe. But let's concentrate on one thing at a time. When you leave here, I imagine you will wish never to see me again,' he growled.

'I imagine so,' she snapped. 'Don't you?' She could hardly believe her ears. Didn't every woman, after she'd been lured into a man's house, dragged into his bedroom and raped?

'Then you realise that we must come to some agreement about the commitments you have already made to the warehouse owners and others. I will not allow you to disappear and go back on your word to them, or to ignore the contracts you have signed. My honour will be tarnished forever. I don't want any of your gutter behaviour in my city. If you double-cross me, I'll destroy you. Slowly. Inch by inch, even if it takes me a lifetime. And I'll take pleasure in your destruction.'

'What? I don't believe I'm hearing this!' she gasped.

'Hannah! Listen to me! You can't let emotions interfere with honour——'

'Wait a minute,' she said, her brain whirling. 'Let me get this straight. You're saying that you want me to put your mind at rest about the imports I've arranged, before...' Her voice trailed away—she couldn't speak of her own rape.

'Of course. Well?' he demanded.

The nerve of the man was incredible! The calculating, cold-blooded... Hannah was lost for words. For several seconds, she searched for a way of expressing her disgust and her disbelief. Khalil's face grew darker with every one of those seconds which passed, and she realised she had to say something or he'd fly into one of his uncontrollable rages. For the moment, at least, he seemed to be calmer.

'Let go of my wrists and I'll tell you exactly what I plan to do,' she said in a low tone.

'Very well.' He slammed the silver-chased bolt across the door and turned the key, slipping it into his pocket. He stood a few paces away from her, his arms folded, his legs straddled. 'Tell me.'

Hannah took a deep breath, the air of sexual menace threatening her vocal chords. 'You know very well I am committed, both here and in London,' she said harshly. 'I can't back out, so you won't lose face with your business colleagues. I need all those purchases I've made. But I want no contact with you, ever again. I'll manage on my own from now on.'

'It will be difficult——'

Her face suffused with anger. 'Not half as difficult as continuing to work with you!' she yelled.

He took a step towards her and she flinched. He went white. 'I'm only going to open the door, Hannah,' he said in a cutting tone.

'But——' She gave an involuntary glance towards his great tented bed.

'Oh, no,' he grated. 'However eager you are, I've lost my appetite.'

She slumped against the door in relief.

'Disappointed?' he sneered. His hand snaked out and cupped her face. 'Beautiful, but rotten to the core,' he breathed. 'You'll have to contain yourself until you get back to Marrakesh. There'll be plenty of men willing to satisfy your hunger. In the meantime...' His head jerked to indicate that they were to leave.

Hardly able to believe her luck, Hannah warily walked out and down the stairs.

'Come into my study,' he said coldly. 'I'll explain to you about bills of transit and all the export requirements.'

In a dream, she followed. To begin with, she barely concentrated on what he was saying, but then she re-alised that he had switched totally to business and had put all thoughts of harming her aside. So she made him go back on what he'd already said, and began to take notes.

It was a long time before everything was settled and she was clear in her mind about everything. But Khalil had been grimly patient and explained well. The complications had been ironed out and she felt quite capable of going ahead on her own.

'Any more questions?' he asked, turning on the lamp by his desk.

Hannah looked around in surprise. She hadn't noticed that it had become dark, nor that they'd been working in the half-light. They must have been very engrossed. How extraordinary. 'No, it's perfectly clear to me.'

His sharp white teeth snagged his lower lip. 'I'll make arrangements for a room to be prepared for you.'

She looked up in alarm. 'I have to stay the night?'

'There's no alternative. I'll never find my way across the *oued*—the river, in the dark. We'll go at first light, I promise.'

'I see. The evening stretches rather long ahead of us, doesn't it?' she said soberly, wondering what on earth they would do with their time.

'There is other entertainment apart from sex, Hannah,' he drawled.

She flushed and shot him a baleful glare. 'I hope you have some books I can read.'

'I'll find you some. But first I must go up for the children's bathtime. Come and say goodnight to them. They will expect it. You needn't stay.'

But she did. The older children were already bathing the younger ones, supervised by two doting women who she imagined must be their nurses from their manner.

Khalil, of course, was greeted by yells of delight and he was soon in the thick of it all, wrestling with slippery soap and even more slippery toddlers, getting his hair covered in suds and his clothes soaked. Hannah didn't like to intrude on what was obviously a family ritual, though she longed to. They were having so much fun. She sat laughing with the two women and later helped to dry the little ones. Her eyes kept flicking over to Khalil.

Saturated, he had eased himself down to the marble-tiled floor and had just enfolded his twin nephews in a vast white bath towel. His head was lowered to their dark ones, his hair plastered in flat curls on his forehead, his lashes wet. He seemed to be telling them a story because the whole room became silent, even the older children listening with breathless excitement.

Each child was dried with tender love. In Khalil's eyes was a vulnerable look—the look of a man whose heart had been given utterly to the innocent love of children. Hannah felt tears well into her eyes. He looked so gentle. Harmless. And the adoration in his eyes hurt her beyond belief, tearing through her defences against him and opening her bruised heart.

Incredibly moved, Hannah helped to carry the sleepy little ones to bed. She watched Khalil bend his handsome head and kiss each drowsy child, watched his black lashes lie thick on his high cheekbones as he murmured something special to every one.

Quietly they both left the last bedroom and Hannah felt as though she'd been put through a wringer. Her emotions were in shreds from the scene of devotion she had just witnessed. One she would never take part in again—and the kind of devotion she would probably never have herself.

'Would you like to come downstairs for a drink?' he asked quietly.

She avoided his soft brown eyes. They'd make her weep. 'A drink would be lovely,' she said brightly.

He sent her on ahead and, when he came down, had changed into a casual white shirt and black trousers. He looked devastating, the golden satin of his neck nestling in the dazzling snowy collar.

The drink helped, but not much. Khalil drank only coffee, thoughtfully stirring the hard knobs of slow-dissolving unrefined sugar, the movement of his graceful hand mesmerising her. She downed her Martini and it was replaced with another.

'I'm afraid it's going to be a quiet evening,' he said. 'I'd better look out some books for you. The television is all in Arabic or French, and so are the videos.'

He found her a handful of paperbacks and left her alone. But she couldn't read. She wandered to the arched window and stared out at the garden, soft with the whirring sounds of cicadas.

'You don't like the books?'

Hannah shook her head at Khalil's voice. 'I can't settle,' she said with a sigh.

'Neither can I.' He'd come closer. 'Do you play backgammon?'

'No.'

'You sound subdued and more than a little bored. It goes against the grain that I am a poor host, even to you. I suggest we have supper and then I'll teach you.'

Listlessly she agreed. Mechanically she ate the spicy soup while Khalil made polite conversation, and then fiddled with a plate of couscous. Gradually, however, as he told her about the history of the extraordinary tribal leaders, she became more interested and forgot her sadness, tucking in quite heartily to the dishes, using the fingers of her right hand as Khalil did and scorning the cutlery placed on the table as a courtesy to her.

He showed her how to roll the rice into a ball in her fingers and eat delicately, with grace. Abdu constantly refilled the copper jug of perfumed water which they had used to wash their hands at the start of the meal.

Trained as a guide, Khalil was full of information and gruesome stories. She became absorbed in the way he spoke, his eyes brilliant with fire as he described the spectacular rise of the Glaoui brothers and the way they had held sway over the surrounding countryside—and had once held greater power than the Sultan himself. It was a tale of murder and corruption, of supreme, absolute rule. And Hannah quailed.

She pushed aside her plate of the almond-filled pastries, the sweet orange-water flavouring suddenly sour in her mouth. 'We're very different, aren't we?' she said quietly. 'Our worlds are so far apart. It's not surprising we don't get on.'

'That's not the reason,' he muttered. 'The history of the English nation—like any other—is one of fierce fighting, lies, deceit, corruption and the struggle for power. People are basically the same, wherever they live. Three of my brothers are married to English women. They are very happy together.' He met Hannah's astonished gaze. 'It's us,' he said morosely. 'We seem doomed to be separated. This will be our last night together, Hannah.'

For once, her eyes were naked and vulnerable as they gazed into his. He seemed unhappy, too.

'We've had one or two good moments together,' she said in a strangled tone.

He nodded solemnly. 'One or two.'

He turned his glass in his hand, his mouth moist from drinking. Hannah's eyes focused on his lips, mesmerised, tempted to go over and... She rinsed her fingers then raised her napkin and wiped her own mouth with slow deliberate movements.

'You said something about backgammon?' she asked, with an attempt at cheerfulness.

He nodded and rose, politely drawing back her chair, ordering coffee from Abdu and leading her into a small, comfortable room lined with soft cushions.

Hannah sank on to them, arranging some for her back, and Khalil sat opposite her, opening up a beautiful wooden board inlaid with different coloured woods.

'This is where you start,' he said. 'The dice dictate your moves——'

'And I make a beeline for the finish,' she said.

'No.' His eyes flickered up to hers. 'It's not that simple. You have choices.' He smiled fleetingly. 'You can stay behind...here...and block any advance by the other player. The novice player runs——'

'I'll block you, then,' she said, meeting his look steadily.

'I thought you might,' he laughed. 'Though everything depends on the throw of the dice. And what you do with your chances,' he murmured.

He explained what he meant, how she could block his approach and prevent him from reaching his goal. And all the time she felt there were hidden messages in what he said. Or perhaps she was searching for them.

'It's a game of risks, some calculated, some dangerous. You can leave yourself exposed and vulnerable, but you must take the consequences,' he said, his eyes dark and watchful.

'I'm used to that,' she sighed.

He made no comment. They began to play and, to her surprise, Hannah was caught up in the excitement of the complicated strategy. She took a risk and left one of her pieces unguarded—he captured it, and captured it with such swiftness that it startled her.

'Beast!' she cried, leaning forward, alert to see if she could get her own back.

'Build up your defences, Hannah. Make them impenetrable. I'm an expert at this game and will get through if you leave so much as one small chink. Don't let me get past, or you've lost.'

The soft silken voice seeped into her mind and body, making her quiver. They weren't close, yet her body felt the pull of his intensely potent sexuality. Effortlessly he could create that electric charge which ran between them, filling the air with danger. Her body throbbed with its current. She felt energised, vitally alive.

Stubbornly she clenched her jaw and scanned the board as she shook the dice. Her luck held out and triumphantly she took one of his pieces.

'Not a wise move,' he breathed. 'I have you.'

'Oh, no!' she protested with a yell.

He laughed, and her eyes gleamed. She'd show him! They began to play in earnest, defending, attacking, always looking for the advantage. She began to have a run of luck, and soon only had one piece left on the board, whereas Khalil had four remaining.

'Expert, eh?' she teased, her eyes dancing. 'What about that, then?'

His slashing grin burnt deep into her body. It was a bitter-sweet moment, finding such enjoyment with him over a simple—no, not simple! It had taken all their powers of guile to reach this point. Hannah grinned confidently back. She was on the homeward run. Nothing could stop her now.

'You won't get me, I'm nearly home,' she crowed.

'My turn, though,' he said, his eyes seeming to glint with inner fires. 'Before you get home anything can happen. All is not lost.'

'Give up,' she jeered. 'Surrender!'

'Never.' He laughed. 'I'd almost forgotten.' His smile died to be replaced by a thoughtful look. 'I'd almost forgotten. There is always a final chance. Destiny has a way of finding its own course.'

Shakily, Hannah forced her eyes down to watch his throw. Her gasp caused him to grin. He had a double six. By the rules of the game, he could remove all four pieces. He had won.

'Oh!' she wailed, laughing. 'The fickle hand of fate! You beast, you rotter, you lucky——'

'Not luck, Hannah. Destiny. It will always lead us to the same point, whatever path we follow, however many detours we make. And I, like a fool, had nearly abandoned all hope, nearly given up.'

'I don't believe it,' she said ruefully. 'I thought I'd won.'

'No. You haven't.'

For some extraordinary reason she was holding her breath. She let it out in a rush. 'I'll beat you next time,' she said shakily, positioning the pieces again.

He laughed and helped her to set up the board. But he won, over and over again, his skill far superior to hers.

'You don't believe in letting me win because I'm your guest, do you?' she said wryly, when he'd beaten her for the sixth time.

'No. I'm trying to make a point.'

Alarmed by the ruthlessness of his voice, she frowned. Suddenly he'd become like a predatory hunter. His whole face looked sensual and aware. She fiddled with the dice. 'That you are a better player than I? Well, you have had more experience,' she said.

'I certainly have. Are you deliberately pretending to be dense?' he murmured.

'I think I'd like to go to bed——'

Hannah stopped short, shocked at the raw desire in his eyes and realising her mistake. The heat crawled up her spine. She wanted him and he must have seen her momentary flash of answering need.

He might be a product of his culture: ruthless, arrogant and chauvinistic, but he had his gentler side. And she half loved, half hated him for that. And wanted—obsessively, desperately.

Khalil smiled, his lips sultry and infinitely inviting to her. 'Defeat into victory,' he said smoothly. 'A successful evening. Goodnight, Hannah. Your room is through that archway, up the stairs and straight ahead. You'll forgive me if I don't escort you.'

'Er...yes. Yes! But...'

'Goodnight!' he snapped, his eyes flashing dangerously.

'Night!' she cried in a high-pitched voice, scurrying out.

CHAPTER EIGHT

IN THE morning, as promised, he drove her back to Marrakesh. They were up early, but that didn't matter. She had hardly slept. Whereas Khalil looked refreshed and infuriatingly handsome.

The flooding rivers and the precipitous roads held no terrors for Hannah any more. She had worse terrors to contend with: those of living without Khalil.

They were silent for most of the journey, and then he suddenly spoke. 'Remember the first time we parted, Hannah?' he asked pleasantly.

She nearly choked with his cruelty. Then remembered that he didn't know what she was feeling. 'When you left because of a family crisis and never returned?' she said in a scathing tone.

'Is that what Dermot said?' he queried, as if that had explained a great deal.

A chill settled inside her. 'Well, you certainly went without saying goodbye to me,' she said, resentment creeping into her voice. 'Of course it was Dermot who told me.'

'He lied. There was no family crisis. I left because he'd made it clear that I'd been moving in on something he regarded as his possession. You. He told me that you and he were lovers when I tackled him about the way you'd looked at him, that time he gave you the ring.'

Her eyes squeezed shut. She didn't want to hear this. She didn't want to know that it had been Dermot who'd ruined her life. 'You didn't have to believe him. I thought you never gave up? That you fought for what you wanted,' she whispered.

'He took care to tell me he was dying,' he said. 'He began to tell me details—personal details—about you and what you . . . he . . .' He ground his teeth savagely. 'I was left in no doubt as to your relationship, Hannah. No man could know such things about a woman and not be intimate with her.'

'You could have said goodbye, you might have told me, even if it was to say what you thought of my morals!' she cried. 'I would have known Dermot had lied, then.'

'What does it matter that he lied about my reason for leaving? I couldn't face you after what I'd heard,' he answered.

'No, I meant——'

'It's past now, Hannah. I left because I believe in cutting off a failed relationship cleanly. Quickly, to give as little pain as possible. I was right to do so. You'd tried to run two lovers at one time and that was something I couldn't accept. I'm a very jealous man, Hannah.'

'You knew what Dermot was like. Yet you believed him! You pushed aside those feelings we'd had for each other——'

'He said you were starved of love, and went for any man,' he said harshly. Hannah's eyes grew huge with horror. 'You were so like my mother, I saw the possibility of that. Her passion for Dermot had consumed him. He'd found it so overpowering that he was in danger of submerging. This is what he told me, and I think that was true. Anyway, the next time we met you were perfectly adjusted to your life, I remember.'

Hannah was about to explain how she felt, but stopped herself in time. Being thought of as Dermot's mistress was perhaps her only defence against Khalil. If he knew she was only an inexperienced virgin, he'd perhaps redouble his attempts to seduce her, thinking that his skill in lovemaking would easily overcome her hesitation. And he'd be right. As it was, he thought she knew it all, and could pick and choose her lovers. She couldn't tell him. He must never know.

'It's such a pity,' he said, as they drove up the little lane to her house. 'I loved you, very much. I've never loved another woman. Well, here you are, then,' he said cheerfully, hauling on the brake.

Stunned, she couldn't move. He opened the door and stretched out his hand. 'Come on, Hannah. Out you get. Journey's over. You're just about home.'

Her hand met his. His touch almost broke her resolve. He'd loved her. *Loved.* Past tense. Her chance had gone, then. He pulled at her hand and numbly she clambered out, her heart heavy.

'Well, well. Stuck for an answer. Right, then,' he said, with a broad grin. 'Bye.'

Her frantic eyes shot up to his. He seemed to be in a devil of a hurry to go.

'I don't know——' she began.

'Try "goodbye".' He smiled.

He didn't care! Not one bit! A croaking sound came from her lips which might have been a farewell, and she turned to hide her face, fumbling with the key. She heard him slam the driver's door and willed her legs to hold her up. Then he drove off without another word.

'Ohhh!' she wailed, unable to unlock the door.

'Are ye havin' trouble, Rapunzel?'

'Oh, Patrick!' she sobbed, turning around and throwing herself into his arms.

'Hey, now, I never knew it was to be my lucky day. Come in with me and I'll make you a real Irish breakfast. It'll put hairs on your chest, sure it will, an' we'll drink tea strong enough to trot a mouse on.'

Hannah was laughing and crying at the same time. 'Oh, I'm so miserable,' she mumbled.

'Are ye? It's a blessing ye said that, or I'd never have known,' he said, firmly moving her into his kitchen. 'The tea's already made. Have a sip. It'll rot your socks.'

Weeping, she obeyed and drew in her breath at the strong taste of tannin. Patrick urged her to finish the cup while he broke eggs into the frying pan.

Over breakfast she told him everything, right from the beginning. Her tears ceased to fall, but her utter depression increased.

'Great writer though he was, and Irish at that, this Dermot seems to have been an out and out bastard,' commented Patrick finally.

'So's Khalil,' she muttered. 'So are all men.'

'I hope you're excluding me from that terrible generalisation.'

'Of course,' she said absently. 'Khalil certainly doesn't live without sex. He's too aware of himself to be celibate. I think he goes for easy women. He thinks I'm worthless,' said Hannah despondently. 'You can't deny that he decided to use me to gratify his sexual appetite.'

'But he didn't,' Patrick pointed out. 'I think you two just strike sparks off each other. The poor man is probably incapable of containing himself. Well, Rapunzel. What are you going to do?'

Tears welled in her eyes again. 'Finish my business here, go home and forget him. I did before, I can do it again.'

'No, you didn't,' said Patrick. 'You kept his memory inside you, waiting, hoping. I don't think you'll ever forget him.'

'You're being a great help,' she said crossly, dabbing at her eyes.

'I think you ought to go for broke. Tell him why you gave those parties and appeared to be having a good time.'

'Why?' she asked listlessly.

'To tie up loose ends. When you get back to London, there'll always be that nagging feeling that he's over here, despising you, when there's no need.'

'I can't risk it!' she cried. 'I'm afraid, Patrick! Afraid he'd——'

'Believe you?' finished Patrick shrewdly. 'Are you frightened that you and he might start one hell of a passion? It's all there, between you, I can see that. Does it bother you, the idea of having him for a lover?'

Hannah squirmed. 'We're not alike. We'll only hurt each other, because of our differences——'

'Well, you'll never know if you don't try. Think about it. I have to go to the Mamounia. My public awaits my tear-jerking rendering of "The Old Rugged Cross". Stay here if you want. I don't mind. We'll talk again when I come back. I'm your friend, Hannah. Lean on me when you want to.'

'Thank you, Patrick,' she said gratefully.

However, Hannah went back to her own house and wandered around, thinking. And while she was thinking, there was a rap on her front door. It was Khalil.

'Come in,' she said before her courage failed her. She'd almost come to a decision.

'I couldn't stay away. I wondered how you were,' he said quietly. 'You've been crying.'

Her hand flew to her face. She must look a terrible sight. It might be a good time to tell him about herself— after all, she could hardly be desirable to him at this moment!

'I've stopped now. I have a lot to say to you. Do you have time to listen?' she asked.

'At last,' he muttered. 'I'll listen.'

They went up to the roof where the softly clacking palm trees filtered the bright sunshine. Hannah didn't know where to start.

'I had the opportunity to tell you this before, but there were reasons why I didn't,' she began. 'I only realised how badly you thought of me when you abducted me——'

'Wait a minute! Have I missed something?' he cried in astonishment. 'Was I asleep during this fascinating adventure?'

She frowned impatiently. 'Don't be amusing at my expense,' she snapped. 'It won't help. You know very well you took me to your house to seduce me, and were intending to rape me if I didn't fall in with your wishes. You even said it wouldn't be an ordeal, that you liked to give your female guests pleasure——'

'Now stop just there!' he said sternly. 'You've got it all wrong! You'd looked nervous; I was trying to re-assure you that meeting my family wouldn't be difficult. And I said nothing about *female* guests. Of course it's my duty to give visitors pleasure when they come to my house! It's the unwritten law of hospitality! I even said I was upset you were being so stand-offish in refusing to meet them——'

'The guards, with rifles...'

He stared at her in exasperation. 'My servants? Hannah, for heaven's sake, you must know that Arab men wander around with rifles. It doesn't mean anything sinister.'

'Khalil... You said you wanted me!'

'Well, I did. Of course I did. I have for years. However, at that moment I also wanted you to meet my brothers and sisters. I'm sure that's what I meant in that particular conversation.' He ran a hand through his hair. 'We seem to have been at cross-purposes, Hannah. I thought you were rejecting my family, you thought you were rejecting my advances.'

'So you weren't dragging me there to satisfy your lust?' she asked shakily.

'Not exactly,' he said with a rueful smile. 'Though I kept wanting to. No wonder you were so rude! No wonder you accused me of filling the house with my whores! Hannah, have you any idea what an insult that was? That's my home! My nephews and nieces stay there often. I wouldn't take a woman of the streets there. Damn it all, I don't deal with women like that anyway!'

'Oh, I'm terribly sorry!' she cried, her eyes pleading. 'Forgive me! But you see how easy it is to misunderstand someone, don't you?'

'Yes. I do. We wasted a day of our lives, Hannah.'

'I've wasted more than that,' she said fervently. With great care, she told him about her relationship with Dermot.

'You told me once that you'd sacrificed everything,' he reminded her quietly.

'I had,' she breathed. 'My chance of personal love.'

'What do you mean?' He frowned.

Hannah sought a defence. Her pride wouldn't let her admit that she loved him. It was too late for that now.

'Oh, I might have met all kinds of men I wanted to marry at that time,' she said casually. 'Dermot kept suitable men away—and so did my supposed reputation.'

'Why should he deliberately allow people to think you were his mistress, if you weren't?' he asked quietly.

'I've been thinking about that. You were right, he was using me. I enhanced his image of the hell-raising writer. He wasn't really like that, Khalil, you must know that!'

'Yes, of course I did. He was a fraud, as I said before. I also know that he was obsessed with his writing and everything else came second. If you're telling me the truth,' he said, with a challenging look, 'how could you stay with him, and let your reputation be ruined?'

'Oh, I loved him, Khalil, as a father; he was all I had, all I could cling on to. He told me, you remember, that he'd tried to stop the publicity about us. I'm not sure that was true, now.'

'The parties were.' Khalil fixed her with a hard stare.

'He needed to forget he was dying. I gave him what he wanted, obliterating the shadow of death by surrounding him with laughter.'

'You have an answer for everything. But not this. I personally saw you in bed with him,' he growled.

'Think back, Khalil! I'm sure he knew it was his last night,' she whispered. 'He was dreadfully afraid and needed comfort, so I hugged him. I'd made him laugh and he collapsed; I fell with him. He was coughing so badly, I didn't dare to move! Oh, I beg you, try to recall what it looked like! Was it a woman making love to a man?'

'I—I suppose not,' he said slowly.

'I swear it was nothing else. Only deep affection.'

Khalil took her hand, searching her eyes. She gazed back, willing him to believe her. It had taken a lot to relive the past.

'You have a great deal of love to give,' he said softly. 'It must have been a blow to you when he died.'

'I was a mental, emotional and physical wreck,' she agreed, her eyes misty. 'I'd been living on my nerves, keeping him going for so long that, when he died and I had no purpose in life, I broke up. I wasn't drunk at the funeral, Khalil! I was heavily sedated—and muddled by one small glass of brandy on top of all that.'

'Hannah,' he whispered. 'I hurt you. I could have been your strength and given you comfort. Instead, I nearly destroyed you with my anger and despair.'

'Despair? You didn't care that much for Dermot.' She frowned.

'You fool!' he said affectionately. 'I'm not talking about him. I cared for you. I cared so much that my passion was only too ready to slide over to hatred.'

'Oh! "Love and hate, no grey",' she said, her eyes wide.

'Precisely. And now we know why he lied, and told me outright that you were his mistress. He was afraid I'd take you from him. I would have done, too.'

'But you believed him,' she said miserably.

'Once, I knew an eighteen-year-old girl with such eager passions that I had to discipline myself severely to avoid our relationship moving too far, too fast,' he said, his mouth sultry as he remembered. 'She was passionate, abandoned. I couldn't be sure how innocent she was; she seemed so confident, sexually. That's why I believed Dermot—that and his...the details he gave. When I saw her again, she was renowned as the cool, sophisticated mistress of a celebrated writer. Her sexuality was under control, but it still blazed out vividly. I hadn't been without women during my absence from you. I hardly imagined you could live close to Dermot, in that house of ill-repute, and stay aloof.'

A deep blush crept over Hannah's skin. 'I wanted to give you everything,' she said simply. 'You misread me. I was uninhibited as a young woman because that's how you made me feel. It's a bit like your house in Marrakesh, Khalil: what you see on the outside isn't necessarily what is on the inside. I've been hiding my real inner feelings for years. It doesn't come easily for me to show them.'

'Imagine what it's like for me.' He smiled. 'I am obsessed with a cold, calculating and brash harlot. And then I see she has another side. Her face is sweet when she looks at children. Her natural good nature is glimpsed in dealing with ordinary people. She is sensible and serious when she is engrossed in talking about business. I see beneath the veils. And I want her, even more.'

Want, she thought sadly. Like his mother, he was consumed with passion. There was no love. He hadn't spoken of that. For her, the situation was almost worse than before. Now that she knew that his departure hadn't been cruel, she had no hatred for him. Instead, she knew that Abdu was right, and the children—Khalil was a good man. A man any woman would want to love.

'Hannah,' he was saying, turning her chin so that she looked into his eyes. 'I know that love is out of the question. But it may grow. We have a great deal we enjoy together, and I can promise you that in bed we will——'

'No, Khalil!' she cried, upset.

'Listen, I'm not making an improper suggestion,' he said urgently. 'I'm asking you to be my wife. Marry me, Hannah. I can't live without you. You possess my mind, my...' He sighed. 'Be my wife. I beg you. We can be happy, I know.'

'Oh, Khalil!' she cried miserably.

His fingers traced the folds of her ear and she quivered.

'See?' he murmured. 'We set up tension between us with the merest touch.'

His lips found her throat and she groaned.

'It's unwise for people from different cultures to marry—— '

'Oh, we in Morocco have been doing that for years,' he muttered, grazing her jaw with his teeth. 'Cleopatra's daughter married a Berber King, two thousand years ago.'

'I'm no Cleopatra——'

'Yes, you are,' he said hotly, his hands catching her shoulders. 'Marry me, Hannah. Marry me.'

'We can't! How can I live here? What about the warehouse, the——'

'These aren't problems. They're excuses. I wouldn't expect you to give up the warehouse idea. It's too exciting and you need to be independent. Life might be a little hectic for us, jetting from one place to another, but we could come to an arrangement to suit each other. As long as I can sleep in your bed,' he growled throatily.

His hand found her breast and the nipple swelled beneath his coaxing fingers. 'I want to make love to you,' he said fiercely. 'I'm dying of need. I don't care about anything else. Think of the pleasure, Hannah. Oh,' he groaned, 'open your mouth, let me kiss you properly.'

Every inch of her body craved him. And she obeyed, responding with shocked arousal to the erotic thrusting of his tongue. She could have him, if she wanted. Not all of him, but enough to weave a fantasy around, to pretend that as his wife she was loved.

No, she couldn't. It would be too painful.

He rocked her with the shudder that ran through his body, coming from his deep, undeniable need. He raised his head and cupped her face, fixing her with his desperate, smouldering eyes.

'Marry me,' he repeated thickly.

'Oh, Khalil!' she moaned, incapable of refusing his molten plea. 'I'll marry you!'

'Hannah!'

His mouth found hers. In that passionate kiss, she was lost, her senses destroying caution. Tenderly he savoured her lips, filling her with sweet intoxication. Hazy, incapable of thinking clearly—not really wanting to—she clung to him.

He was shaking, his hard, roving hands trembling at their fingertips. His body became insistent, his breathing fierce and hot. 'You're driving me mad with desire,' he said hoarsely. 'I'll have to leave now or take you.'

'Leave,' she whispered.

'No,' he groaned. 'I can't! I've only just won you!'

Hannah froze inside. Was she, then, a prize in a game? Had he set out to master her as he had mastered the game of backgammon? 'You must leave, Khalil,' she rasped.

His tousled head lifted reproachfully. 'I don't have to, now we're virtually engaged. What do you think, my darling?' he coaxed.

'No!' she said sharply, turning away and biting her lip.

Whatever his reason for wanting her, she couldn't deny herself by going back on her acceptance of marriage. She'd spent so many years loving him, so many years without affection. His passion was enough, and, as he said, he might learn to love her. She'd be a good wife to him. Hannah refused to allow her other voice to infiltrate her mind. But somewhere, she knew, it was warning her. It was trying to tell her she was deluding herself.

'I'm sorry,' he muttered. 'Forgive me. I take one look at you and everything inside me explodes. You're walking dynamite, Hannah!'

She emerged from her semi-paralysis. 'I need a little time——'

'Yes. I think I do, too.' He grinned. 'Time to cool down and make a few plans. We'll have plans, too. There's a lot to iron out. The first thing is for me to organise a party at my house in the mountains and make a formal announcement. Tuesday.'

Hannah nodded, numb with the effect of her decision, her mind frantic. What had she done?

'I'll keep away from you today,' said Khalil, his eyes devouring her body hungrily. 'And meet you tomorrow somewhere very public.' He laughed. 'Otherwise I can't guarantee I'll keep my hands to myself. How about the Mamounia, for lunch at noon?'

'Fine,' she said faintly. When her brain started to work again, she'd be able to think properly.

'Don't go talking to any men in the meantime,' he said, pulling her to her feet. 'You belong to me now.'

His long, lingering kiss made her sway helplessly in his arms. Against his powerful magnetism she was defenceless. Her hands slipped up to the smooth nape of his neck and her body moulded itself to his.

He threaded his hands through her hair, drawing her harder into him until it was as if she knew every part of his body intimately, every beautiful, flexed muscle.

'Oh, Hannah!' he groaned. 'How can I ever wait for our wedding? I'm leaving, before I consummate our betrothal here and now.'

Hannah sank unsteadily into a chair when he'd gone. It had all happened so quickly... She'd only meant to set the record straight, and she'd ended up by agreeing to marriage! Was she being stupid? It seemed she didn't know her own mind any more. If only she could talk to someone...

Patrick! He'd lived here a long time, he might be able to consider her behaviour dispassionately, whereas she...

She was hopelessly in love. Every time she pictured Khalil, her heart came to a grinding halt. And, so it appeared, did her brains. She'd see if Patrick could spare her a moment between performances—she certainly couldn't wait until he came back.

The bus journey took some time. There was a hold-up at the police check ahead, and the passengers on the bus steamed in the heat as they waited.

Eventually she was walking up the wide marble steps of the most expensive hotel in Morocco, the legendary Mamounia Hotel. It was a vast place, and she kept wandering into little courtyards and bird-filled gardens instead of bumping into singing Irishmen.

Then she found herself in a corridor which led to a number of ground-floor bedrooms, each with its own individual light above the door, and just beyond was a bar. She was about to walk in and ask the barman if he knew where Patrick was, when she saw Khalil there with his back to her. And she suddenly remembered with a sickening lurch of her heart that Khalil had been enjoying the sexual favours of another woman, all the time he was being frustrated in his desire to master *her*.

Because he wasn't alone. There was the young blonde, tucked against his shoulder, embraced by his arm. And he was looking down at her and laughing. Hannah reeled back, shrinking against the doorway. The woman was sensationally beautiful and wearing a bikini beneath a white towelling wrap embroidered with the letter 'M'.

Hannah couldn't move. Her haunted eyes saw that Khalil and the woman were getting up from the bar and the girl was surreptitiously handing him her room key. It seemed that Khalil was being furtive, too, because he quickly slipped it into his pocket and they parted. Her stomach an empty void, Hannah slipped quickly behind a potted banana plant, terrified that Khalil should see her. She wanted to feel in control of herself and right now all she felt was a terrible nausea, which was choking her. Oh, God! He must be the biggest *bastard* in Africa!

Furiously subduing her thudding heart, she peered around the plant. Khalil had gone along the corridor and was unlocking one of the doors. No doubt Miss M. would be along in a moment, she thought miserably.

'Miss Jordan?'

She jumped and her hand flew to her mouth to stifle a gasp. A slim, fair young man with a notebook in his hand was standing beside her.

'What do you want,' she asked, irritably.

'It is Miss Jordan, isn't it?' he asked with a pleasant smile.

Hannah was in no mood for charming men. She was in no mood for men at all. 'Yes.' She turned away.

'Please don't go. Frankie sent me. She's been trying to get hold of you for a day or so. I couldn't believe my eyes when I saw you.'

'Frankie? Oh, lord! I'd forgotten...'

Hannah tried to pull herself together. Her work was all she had left now. Oh, God! she thought in despair. Her life *was* a series of dramas! A proposal and an unfaithful lover, all in the space of an hour or so. The rat! The evil, hypocritical——

'You seem a bit agitated...'

'What do you want?' she asked curtly.

'I'm Steve Anderson. I write biographies. I'm doing one on Dermot O'Neill——'

'God!' croaked Hannah, hurrying away.

'No, please, you don't understand,' cried the writer, catching up with her and grabbing her arm urgently. 'I want to exonerate you. Frankie sent me!'

Hannah's slowly working brain jolted into gear. 'What?' she cried, catching hold of his lapels. 'What did you say?'

'I want your side of it,' said Steve gently, looking at her with compassion. 'I know what you went through. She told me. I'm not out to produce a lurid story, just the truth. That's what biographies should be. Will you agree to talking to me?'

Hannah shut her eyes. If she did it would be all over then, and her soul could rest in peace. 'Yes. Oh, yes,' she breathed.

'Wonderful! When?'

To her embarrassment, she saw that she was still clutching him and she let go, blushing. 'I'm sorry,' she said shakily. 'I—I had rather a shock just before you came. I can't talk to you for a while.'

'Oh, dear. It's a bit urgent. My deadline is up and I was only getting a bit of extra background when I discovered that your role in Dermot's life wasn't what we all thought. I've only got three days in Marrakesh and then I have to return. I'd hoped... I'm sorry, I'll have to forget it,' he said regretfully. 'Damn! Oh, well. That's life. I'll scratch a few facts together from what Frankie's told me, since you're not feeling up to it——'

'Wait.' Hannah steadied her breathing, clenching her stomach muscles as she did so in order that the sickness there would go away. It was time she cleared the slate. Only her own version would ring true, that she wasn't Dermot's mistress. Without facts, figures and explanations that Frankie didn't have, the Press would be raking the whole thing up, discussing the half-hearted denials when the book was published, and she'd relive the whole damn thing again.

'I could meet you this evening,' he said hopefully.

She heaved a huge sigh. What else did she have to do? 'Yes. All right. I'll do my best. Here?'

He looked bashful. 'I was only rubber-necking, Miss Jordan,' he said wryly. 'My hotel is much less expensive. How about the Café Renaissance? I hear there's a terrific view from the roof.'

Hannah spent the rest of the day wandering aimlessly in the Menara Gardens, trying to put her life back together again. Marrying Khalil was out of the question. Before, she'd been prepared to accept that he didn't love her, but she had thought he'd been honest when he'd said his need for her was great. He didn't need her at all. She was merely another conquest, whose price had been marriage.

Her stupid brain had completely forgotten his infidelity. Dully she realised that she was turning to ice again inside. Khalil was right—destiny did have an uncanny knack of driving you in the same direction, no matter how you tried to divert it. Her destiny was never to find love. For her, it was all a mirage after all.

Summoning all her strength, she went to Khalil's office.

'He's not here,' said his male secretary, looking a little harassed. 'I think there's a crisis somewhere.'

'Can you get a message to him urgently?' she asked, feeling defeated. She had to cut Khalil out of her life and start again. Bounce. She prided herself on that. 'Tell him I need to speak to him. I'll be at home—oh, or at the Café Renaissance after seven this evening.'

Bounce, she told herself on the way home. So she washed her hair and made up her face, and went for Power Dressing again. The last time she'd done that, she thought unhappily, had been on her arrival in Marrakesh. A defence against Khalil. The armour had gone on again and she was erecting barriers to protect herself.

All through her interview with Steve, she sat waiting for Khalil to phone. He never did. A group of Moroccans came up to the roof on the crowded sixth floor of the café, sat very near them and stared rather hard at her, but that was all.

She and Steve sat closely together, trying to hear one another above the noise, blotting out their surroundings and concentrating hard on getting as much done as possible.

'It's gone midnight,' she said finally, checking her watch.

Steve put his hand on hers and gave her a grateful look. 'It's been wonderful,' he said happily. 'You're an incredible woman. I can promise you'll be glad you gave me a little of your time.'

'Give it all you've got, Steve,' she smiled wistfully. 'Make it good.'

'I'll get a *petit taxi*,' he said.

Hannah followed him past the fascinated Moroccans on the next table, smiling wryly as she wondered what they'd made of the conversation.

Steve accompanied her and then said goodbye. She hadn't minded giving him the time. It was all finished— he had all the material he wanted. Besides, spending the evening with him had helped to postpone the awful moment when she would be alone again.

There was no message from Khalil at home. That night she worked on her accounts, shutting all thoughts of him from her mind whenever they tried to penetrate her mechanically working brain.

Knowing she must get all her business done and leave Marrakesh as soon as possible, she scythed an efficient, brisk path through the *souks* in the morning, ordering bolts of cloth, brass and copperware, baskets, cosmetics, dyes, perfumes...

She was hard, tough, immovable. Her sharp, steely bartering didn't go down well but she had to fill her day and the late evening hours. Still there was no message. During the day, she contacted his office. They hadn't heard from him, either. She began to worry. And then the penny dropped.

Of course. He was rolling around in bed with the blonde in the hotel. Hannah's eyes darkened as the pain spurted in a hot flood through her entire body. God! She was a fool! She did still love him!

Grimly she bought shoes, slippers, handbags. Spices, herbs, jewellery. Any spare time was spent in arranging shipment and organising storage in the warehouse with Frankie. For a few hours each night she fell into a heavy, dreamless sleep of exhaustion.

And then she realised, waking very late one morning with a sudden shock, that the man who was standing on her doorstep and ringing her bell so loudly must be from Khalil.

When she opened the door, he handed her a note: 'Hassan will drive you to my home. I await you there.'

Dishevelled and tired, she stared at Hassan numbly. He bowed politely, touching his hand to his heart, and went to wait in the car.

Feeling cold and anaesthetised against emotion, she dressed with trembling fingers. Her most elegant suit, kept in case of a special occasion. Wide shoulder-pads, narrow waist, flounced skirt to the jacket. Short, slender skirt. Bright poppy-red. Black stiletto shoes. Strong eye make-up and lipstick to hide her pallor. Huge silver earrings and plenty of bracelets.

She looked at herself in the mirror, the clothes at odds with her dispirited face and body. 'Bounce, damn you!' she grated. 'Don't let him know you care. Keep your pride, if nothing else!'

She picked up her bag and locked the door. It was like going to her own funeral, to tell Khalil she never wanted to see him again, that she would never be his wife. Because she could easily keep quiet and say nothing. It was tempting, she mused, thinking of the way he would make love to her. Though, she admitted ruefully, he'd be making love to other women as well. If he only loved her a little... He could have lied, instead of being so open about his feelings for her!

, Her mind drifted, swaying back and forth like a weathercock. The car swung sharply around the corner and she looked up.

'Hassan! This isn't...' Her voice trailed away as Hassan nodded encouragingly at her. They were driving into the mountains; Khalil had meant his *mountain* home, whereas she'd thought he'd naturally be working in Marrakesh, taking a brief break from the energetic blonde in the hotel.

This would be awkward. She'd be obliged to ask him to make sure that she got home again. Or... A frightening thought struck her. Maybe he'd be so enraged at her rejection of him that he'd take what he'd always wanted, then and there. It would be his final, destructive blow. And he'd warned her of his vengeance.

CHAPTER NINE

THE LONG, gruelling journey took its toll on Hannah. By the time they swept up to Khalil's stronghold, nerves had made her irritable and jumpy. And when she saw the chaotic scene around the great house, she felt her temper rising too.

There were donkeys, mules, cars, horses, ponies and trucks outside. The place thronged with people, dressed in all kinds of costume from elegant European to exotic oriental. For a moment she thought it must be a fancy-dress party, and then she gave a groan. Khalil had gone ahead with the party. It must be Tuesday!

Feeling slightly sick, Hannah stepped from the car and came face to face with Khalil himself. They stared at one another for several seconds and Hannah wondered wildly if he knew why she'd come, because his eyes were hard and cold. But then he bent and kissed her lightly on both cheeks. Her hands rested briefly on his crisp white *djellaba* and then she jerked back as if she were touching hot coals.

For Khalil burned. His heart thudded violently. And she saw from under her lashes that his hands were shaped into fists.

'Well,' he drawled. 'I don't know about absence making the heart grow fonder, Hannah, but it's done something spectacular to the body. You look very sexy. What *have* you been doing?'

'I—I—I must talk to you,' she said huskily.

'Sure. I have every intention of getting you alone,' he said, his eyes telling her exactly why.

'Khalil, this is important——'

Suddenly she was surrounded by the children. They swept her along to their parents and she was introduced to Khalil's brothers and sisters. Their friendly, warm welcome was a farce. She struggled to keep her head above water and keep her dignity intact.

'Poor Hannah!' laughed Sue, one of the English wives, resplendent in an elegant Parisian suit. 'You look utterly bewildered. I promise you, it gets better. Come on, I'll take you around.'

'I must speak to Khalil! Where is he?' cried Hannah, frantically searching.

He seemed to be embracing some new arrivals. All pretty women, wearing fantastic Berber jewellery. He was pretending to examine an elaborate head-dress, as the pretext for stroking a young woman's hair. Her heart sank.

'He's greeting his guests. Fatma's wearing a new head-dress. Fab, isn't it? Look, we're roasting sheep,' prattled on Sue. 'Traditional pit ovens. Gorgeous roast, better than the Sunday joint.'

She cracked a joke in Arabic with the men basting the meat. Its herby, aromatic smell mingled with the fragrance of spices and incense, but Hannah felt like retching.

'How long have you been married?' she asked faintly, fighting down the nausea.

'Seven years. Those are my two dots of humanity, over there,' said Sue, pointing to a toddler and a baby being joggled in the air by a wild-looking tribesman. Wild, that was, apart from his face. That was soft, like the faces of all Moroccan men when they eyed the 'fruit of life'.

'Don't you miss England?' Hannah asked hesitantly.

'I was there last week. It was pouring with rain! I know what you're worrying about. There are differences, sure, but this is a pretty cosmopolitan country. And a super climate!' She grinned. 'Besides, the ben Hrima have a long tradition of powerful women. Some of them have ruled over other villages. My husband and I live as we want to. It's not restrictive. Berber woman have long eaten with men, gone without the veil and been their equals.'

'But you've become a Muslim?'

'Oh, no. We got married in England and I became a resident here. That's all. You don't even lose your passport, or your nationality, Hannah. Don't worry. You can be as independent as you like.'

'Apart from having endless children?' she asked cynically.

'Now, who's been telling you stories?' chided Sue. 'I keep saying: you do what you like. I'm sticking at two. I can't spend my life having babies. I've got a school to run.'

'A school?'

'Mmm. Don't you think Khalil's cousin Shade is a doll?'

Hannah followed Sue's nod. She swayed a little. He was gazing in adoration as a dark-eyed girl of about sixteen gesticulated furiously, ending her excited chatter with a wild, exuberant movement which had Khalil roaring with laughter.

'Absolute scream,' said Sue. 'She wants to be a comedienne on television.'

Hannah felt dazed. Around her was a medieval world. And, if the cars and clothes were anything to go by, a highly sophisticated one, too. She found it hard to accept that the women were so forward, so liberated. No wonder the men managed to satisfy themselves... She decided to question the ever-willing Sue.

'I—I understood the men in this country have a leaning towards infidelity,' said Hannah, her throat dry and harsh.

'Well, you needn't worry about that. Khalil is above suspicion.' She laughed. 'Hey, Khalil!'

'No, please——' Hannah groaned.

'Prove to Hannah what you think about her,' said Sue in a stage whisper. 'She's got nerves.' She laughed and disappeared hurriedly into the crowd.

'Nerves, Hannah?' he murmured silkily.

'Khalil, can't we go somewhere private?' Hannah begged.

He smiled, but even to Hannah's confused mind it was obvious that the smile never reached his eyes. They were black and hard. He caught her around the waist possessively, his mouth twisting.

'You're insatiable!' he muttered. 'You just can't get enough, can you?'

She blinked. 'Khalil!' she said, shocked.

Before she could say anything more, she was being introduced to some of his friends. From then on, they were never alone. It was a terrible situation. Everyone fully expected them to make an announcement about their marriage after the feast. Hannah felt as if she was going mad. She even thought she saw the blonde from the hotel, and pushed through the chattering guests in an attempt to confront the woman.

'Looking for Khalil?' asked one of his brothers, as she brushed past. 'Ah, you'll have to watch yourself, Hannah! He's already chasing another lovely blonde!'

'I know,' she said grimly, hurrying on.

Even his family had seen! How could he be so blatant!

'Want something, Hannah?' came Khalil's husky voice, close behind her. He pulled her into his body and wrapped his arms around her, her spine pressed hard against him.

Several guests smiled at them both, and she suffered his embrace with lowered eyes. She twisted her head so that he could hear her. 'The rumour is that I'm not the only blonde you've been after,' she said brightly.

'True. Excuse me. I think I see her.'

She was abandoned, stunned. With good intent, his family and friends buttonholed her, making her feel more and more of a heel. They were all so friendly and she'd have to let them all down. They seemed absolutely delighted that she and Khalil were to announce their betrothal. It filled her with despair that their relationship was hardly a secret to anyone. He must have told them all. Why?

She *must* stop this. Yet every time she marched decisively over to Khalil he melted into the crowds. And, before she knew it, they were all making their way to the large arena where the fantasia was to be held, and which was piled high with carpets and cushions.

Hannah felt her arm being taken and Khalil was drawing her down. They were close enough for her to take her chance and tell him—to end the ridiculous charade.

'Khalil, we can't marry——'

'I wasn't intending that we should,' he said lazily. 'This announcement is to paper over the cracks. Have some bread. Your mouth's open.'

'I—I——' She shut it. Then tried again, her voice croaking. 'Why have *you* changed your mind? I——'

'The incident in the Mamounia Hotel changed my mind,' he breathed. 'Infidelity does amazing things to one's desire.'

'Oh!'

So the other woman had given him everything he wanted. He had no need of her now. Although she'd known that, it still came as a shock. Her life had become a vacuum.

'"Oh"? No further comment?'

'I've got to get out of here,' she muttered.

'Try it and I'll make you regret it,' he murmured, his lips close to her ear. 'And, if my family ever suspects that we are deadly enemies now, you will pay for it later. Understand?' He leant away again, a pleasant smile on his face.

'But . . .'

He pretended to nuzzle her jaw. 'Act, Hannah. Act as you never have before. You can do it. Some of these people have driven for two days to reach my house. It is an important time. You won't spoil the occasion.'

'You said——'

'We announce our engagement, we celebrate. We act like the perfect, loving couple.' His mouth kissed the tips of her fingers.

'Oh, God!'

'Then, a little later,' he continued, kissing her throat, 'we quietly announce that the wedding will not take place. Kiss me.'

'I——'

He caught hold of her hand and crushed it. She met his eyes, and saw the venom there. *Love and hate.* He intended to destroy her.

'Kiss me.'

With an attempt at a sultry look, she obediently lifted her head. He made no move. She was forced to put her hand to his face and bring his head down to hers. The kiss fired her loins, mocking her body with its sensuality.

'Keep smiling,' he breathed, placing his arm around her.

Like a stupid doll, she smiled. He'd suffer for this, she vowed. For every ghastly second.

'The occasional caress might be in order,' he drawled.

Gritting her teeth, she put on her act. He wanted a doting girlfriend, he'd get one. She fluttered her eyelashes and pouted alluringly all through the interminable meal.

The courses went on and on. Soups, spiced meats— Hannah barely knew what she was eating. Every scrap tasted the same. Except the morsels which Khalil fed to her. They were poison and it was all she could do not to gag on them because her throat was blocked by a seemingly solid lump.

And, relentlessly, the male and female dancers shuffled around the seated groups, the drums beating out a monotonous rhythm, cymbals clashing, a spine-tingling and shrill cry soaring above the plaintive chanting. The primitive ululations electrified the air, making both herself and Khalil tense their bodies.

The slide of his hand over her waist weakened her. The hard jut of his hip pressed against her. His eyes were constantly on her and the movement of his fingers drummed a slow, steady rhythm that accelerated the beat of her pulse. He was making love to her with his eyes.

In a trance, she stared at him, transfixed.

'You are the most exciting woman I've ever known,' he muttered hoarsely.

'I—I——' She'd lost her bounce. She pretended to cough.

He gently thudded her back and then his hand trailed down her spine, bone by bone. She must fight back.

At the end of the meal, rose petals were showered on them and huge sprays of fragrant white broom were laid on the ground till the very breeze blew with their rich scent. Khalil broke a piece from a sugar cone and popped it into her mouth, to the applause of those near. She had initially recoiled at the touch of his fingers on her lips, but his glittering eyes had made her open her mouth for him and his fingers had lingered, torturing her beyond all endurance.

'Are you finding this a bit of a strain?' he whispered.

Keep punching, she told herself. Don't let him know you're flat on the canvas from a knock-out blow. With a supreme effort, Hannah gritted her teeth and forced a wide-eyed look, hoping she sparkled convincingly. 'Who, me? Hard-hearted Hannah?' she said, arching her brow.

He laughed harshly. 'You don't give a damn, do you?'

'Not a damn,' she agreed perkily.

He subsided, turning his back to talk to the others. She felt a slight relief from the intense pressure she'd been under. They drank coffee, everyone lounging, laughing, fathers idly caressing their children. She noticed Khalil's harrowed expression as he watched one of his brothers as he tickled his little son.

She made her heart as hard as steel.

The groups were mixing now, wandering around, gossiping with each other. Hannah wondered if she could get up and find somewhere in the house to be alone for a while. Then she saw the beautiful young blonde coming towards Khalil and her heart thudded like a steamhammer. With a muttered exclamation, he jumped up and ran over to her as if he couldn't wait to see her. Hannah's shocked eyes took in the triple kiss they exchanged and then she turned away, sick to her stomach.

She rose and began to wander through the crowds, acknowledging smiles, outwardly glittering and vivacious, inwardly dying. To her surprise, she found herself in the inner gardens of the house. The noise of the party was deadened by the high surrounding walls and she felt that for a moment she could find a little peace of mind and have a chance to summon up her energy for the strain to come.

The sound of someone calling disturbed her and she moved away wearily, not wanting anyone to find her and intrude on her solitude.

'Hannah! Where are you?'

Reluctantly she stepped into the open. 'Can't you leave me alone?' she snapped.

'We should be announcing our engagement,' he said coldly.

'I don't think I can go through with it,' she retorted. 'Say what you like to them. I can't be a hypocrite.'

'That's rich, coming from you,' he said savagely, his eyes black with hatred. 'You lied to me! You pretended to be the injured innocent, that you'd been wrongly accused of being Dermot's woman. Instead, you're as cheap and immoral as I first imagined.'

'I don't know what you're talking about,' she said haughtily. 'And while we're talking about hypocrites, I might say that you are the most brilliant master of deceit, to be able to fool so many people. Everyone I know seems to think you're as pure as the Atlas snow, whereas I know for a fact you're as dirty as the floor of a donkey park!'

'I? Be careful what you say. Don't be ridiculous——'

'If that's your only defence, you'd better run and hide,' she said vigorously. 'Because I'm going to open a few eyes. Starting with your family and the exact relationship between you and that young blonde you've been chasing all day. How they can be so blind, I don't know.'

'She's my niece,' snapped Khalil.

'Yes, so you said,' she scorned.

'My brother's daughter,' he growled.

'I don't believe you,' she said. 'She must be eighteen at least. And you've been all over her.'

'My eldest brother,' he said through clenched teeth. 'There are twenty years between us! Lalla is——'

'Oh, Lalla, is it?' she said sarcastically. 'Well, why would our dear little Lalla be wearing a towelling robe in the Mamounia Hotel with the letter M on the pocket?'

'Because it's a hotel robe,' he snapped.

'Oh, very good,' she said, applauding politely. 'Does your brother know his daughter gives you her room key and arranges secretly to meet her uncle?'

'You and your evil mind!' he snarled. 'You would think the worst of me! Go to the hotel! You'll find everyone wandering around the pool in those robes!'

'Why Lalla, though? What's she doing in a hotel in Marrakesh? Why wasn't she at home with her father? Answer me that!' she flung at him, half hysterical.

'My brother lives in Paris. Lalla works in the Mamounia. If, as I assume, you saw me take her key, then it was for her room. The senior management staff have bedrooms on the lower corridor.'

'You actually admit——'

'I admit I went there, yes,' he snapped. 'Of course we were discreet! She couldn't be seen handing me her key in public.'

'If you're her uncle?' she said in a disbelieving tone.

'People,' he said with a vicious snarl, 'tend to jump to the wrong conclusions, and I wasn't going to embarrass her. She's a beautiful girl and even uncles are not supposed to be alone with their teenage nieces. She wanted her sunglasses. I imagine you were spying on us. If you'd watched a little longer you would have seen me go to her room and come out again. I joined her at the pool and we discussed a mad idea she had for organising a firework display with two hearts entwined.'

'I—I can check this, you realise——'

'Oh, curse you, Hannah!' he roared. 'Check it all you like! Lalla is a child! I've been trying to get hold of her ever since she arrived here, to see if she had set up that display in defiance of me. I wanted it cancelled, if so. I couldn't stand the irony of it all.'

'You didn't make love to her?' she said, gulping.

He gave her a strange look. 'Curse you, Hannah! I haven't made *love* to any woman,' he said throatily. 'I've only ever loved you.'

Hannah stopped breathing. Her lashes flickered up and saw that he looked drawn and anguished. Her head spun. Could she be wrong? Was everyone else right and...

'I'll go and tell everyone to go home,' he muttered.

'Why did you tell *me* we weren't getting married?' she asked, quaking.

He gave a derisive laugh. 'The irony of the situation is hard to take,' he rasped. His harrowed face scanned Hannah's. 'How you can stand there so innocently, I don't know. The game's up, Hannah. I saw you in the arms of a man in the hotel. And don't tell me it was your nephew. I'm gullible where you're concerned, but not that stupid.'

He turned away. Hannah's mind flew to the incident with Steve in the hotel foyer. She'd put her hands on his shoulders...

'Wait, Khalil,' she began.

He stopped, his head tipping back in anguish. 'Don't,' he groaned. 'Don't lie. I'd rather you admitted it. You like men. I've been a fool not to admit that to myself. You see, I tried to find you. All that afternoon you were missing. That evening you met that man and talked like lovers at the Café Renaissance. My friends saw you. They were sure it was you. There aren't many women in Marrakesh like the notorious Hannah Jordan. I'd described you to them in——' he laughed mirthlessly '—in minute detail. They also described the man to me. It was the same one. I know what you've been up to.'

'I see,' she said quietly. 'You believe I've been spending the last few days in bed——'

'Don't say it!' he cried, despair thickening his voice. He whirled around, his face white with strain. 'You've won this one, Hannah. Oh, you've proved to me that I'm an innocent compared with you when it comes to playing dirty. I thought I'd teach you a lesson, and ruin you at first. Then I decided it would be more amusing to seduce you.' He frowned angrily. 'Then I discovered that the joke had backfired. I wanted you, and despised myself for that—especially when I found myself assaulting you like a hungry animal. You've got through my defences, you've wriggled through every pore and invaded my body more surely than any Roman, Vandal, Arab, Spaniard or Frenchman! I, descended from a long line of proud, free men, have been devoured by a female Casanova. I'm free no more. I think, eat, sleep, dream of you. Every line of your body entices me. Every beat of my heart is thudding out your name, every breeze from the mountains brings to me the perfume of your breath, the softness of your body. Go!' he roared. 'Get out of my sight!'

He shook with passion. Hannah's heart was singing. Her face became radiant as Khalil's words dinned into her senses. He loved her. He really did. And all their troubles had been created by fear, and a refusal to believe that their love was more than a fragile, tenuous thread, ready to snap at any pressure.

She knew what she had to do. This was her time for taking risks, for making a life-choice. For taking the hand of destiny and running with it, instead of against it. It had led her this far. She must take the final step herself. Yet she needed a little strategy to overcome his hatred. And he needed proof.

'But Khalil, I want you,' she said simply, undoing her jacket buttons slowly, her eyes upon him.

He closed his eyes and groaned.

'Before we part... Why deny yourself?' she husked. 'Look at me, Khalil. Take what you want. We'll both enjoy it.'

Beneath her jacket she wore a thin silk sun-top, whose narrow straps had meant that she couldn't wear a bra. The red silk clung to her breasts, magnifying them. Khalil's eyes had lifted to her thrusting nipples.

She smiled. She had him.

She dropped the jacket and stroked the curve of her hip. A hard, venomous anger spread over Khalil's face and for a moment she was really frightened, realising she was playing with fire. He might her hurt badly.

'Khalil, I——'

He advanced on her retreating form, his face proud. 'I wouldn't take you, if you were the last woman in the world,' he seethed.

'Oh!'

Her face crumpled while he looked at her in astonishment. The tears ran in never-ending floods down her face, all her despair and misery released like the melting snows.

'Don't cry,' he said roughly.

'I c-c-can't help it!' she sobbed. 'I l-l-love you! I tried not to and I kept finding reasons not to and I kept telling myself you weren't everything you were cracked up to be and——'

A burst of weeping prevented her from continuing. Khalil put his arms around her and she wept on his warm shoulder while he patted her back.

'We both seem to have become victims,' he said wryly.

'Hold me, Khalil!' she choked. 'If it's only for the last time, hold me!'

She raised her wet face to his and he frowned, bringing out a handkerchief and dabbing at her eyes, his jaw clenched hard. His fingers became slower in their movements, almost mechanical, and all the while she stared at him with pleading eyes, willing him to kiss her.

'Hannah,' he said thickly, his mouth soft and sultry.

Her face moved imperceptibly towards his and then she was being swung boldly into the air. Khalil was striding purposefully into the house. She nestled in his arms, nuzzling up to his throat, running her teeth enticingly along the line of his beard.

He flung her on his bed and his relentless mouth was driving into hers, his merciless hands beginning to strip the clothes from her body.

She reached up, ripping at his shirt. She was melting, a hot pool of liquid beneath his hands, flowing with him.

'Oh, Khalil,' she whispered. 'I love you.'

'And I love you,' he growled. 'May I be cursed forever because of it, but I love you and can never let you go. Whatever your past. I will brand you as mine, Hannah,' he said, ripping off her top. 'You'll never want another man again, never desire another. Only me. And I'll keep you locked up, here in my room!'

She couldn't think. His mouth was doing indescribably erotic things to her body, his hands still working to remove every stitch of clothing. And she helped. Her back arched up and she wriggled out of her skirt, allowing him to slide down her tiny red briefs.

'Oh, you're beautiful,' he murmured huskily. 'Every inch of you. I knew you would be.'

His dark head swept down her body. The knives of aching need ripped through her and he stared at her for one long, tense moment. Then he slowly removed his own clothes, Hannah's eyes dark with longing as inch by inch his beautiful golden body was revealed to her.

'Now, Hannah,' he breathed, his heated skin scorching hers as he covered her. 'Now I take my pleasure. After that, I give you yours. But mine first,' he said savagely. 'You've driven me to this! Every flirtatious glance,' he snarled, his fingers sliding to her thighs and making her moan with their ruthless delight. 'Every sway of your body.'

She began to utter little noises in her throat, catching at his shoulders and digging in her nails at the exquisite sensations. 'Oh, stop, please, I can't bear it!'

'You like it,' he growled. 'And I'm far too hungry to stop. Your lesson, Hannah. I am the master.'

Then his knee parted her legs and she gasped in fear, but his hands slid beneath her back and raised her, driving her hard on to him. She screamed with shock at the fierce sharp pain as he thrust into her body, filling her, and he froze like a stone statue as she lay rigidly beneath him.

'Hannah!'

'Khalil.' She trembled, her voice cracking. Her body relaxed. She feared nothing. He loved her. 'Take me. I want you to be the first.'

'I——' He couldn't speak.

She moved. Slowly, gently, cautiously, finding it gave her pleasure. And he moved, too, slowly, gently, cautiously, giving her more pleasure. His lips touched hers tenderly, and, like a long-drawn-out celebration of their love, they drove themselves towards a crescendo, matching each other, touch for touch, kiss for kiss, passion for passion.

Finally he moved within her faster and faster till she thought she was losing her mind, and between them they reached that highest moment of sharing.

They lay together afterwards, tangled naked limbs, hot, steamy, content. It must have been a long time before Hannah could raise the energy even to smile. She didn't need to—her whole body was in ecstacy.

Khalil rolled over and raised himself on one elbow, looking at her in a bemused way. 'You should have said. You should have *said*, Hannah!' he groaned.

'I did,' she mumbled.

'I mean, just now. Before...' He bit his lip.

'You wouldn't have believed me,' she said.

'No,' he answered hoarsely. 'No one would imagine that such a desirable, sexy, sensual woman could be——' he shook his head in disbelief '—a *virgin*! I can't... If I hadn't... Oh, Hannah!' he cried in confusion. 'Forgive me!'

'Only if you promise not to keep me locked up.' She grinned.

'Locked up? I want the world to know you're my wife. I take it you will marry me now?' he laughed.

'We could announce our engagement today,' she said, giggling. 'I think there's a party going on out there for that very purpose.'

He clapped a hand over his forehead. 'I'd forgotten! There must be five hundred people, wondering where we are!'

'No,' she said, shaking her head. 'They probably know where we are.'

'In that case,' he murmured, his eyes softening with desire again, 'they can wait a bit longer.'

'Khalil!' she protested, as he reached out for her. She put on a prim expression. 'We must attend to our guests. It's a matter of courtesy. Honour.'

'Are you teasing me? You learn too quickly, that's your trouble,' he complained. 'Maybe in thirty years or so you'll even be beating me at backgammon.'

'In thirty years, you might be a grandfather,' she said smugly.

'What a fate,' he whispered, abandoning his duty to his guests once more. 'What a wonderful, wonderful fate.'

No more a mirage. It had been their own Night of Destiny.

**THIS JULY, HARLEQUIN OFFERS YOU
THE PERFECT SUMMER READ!**

Sunsational

EMMA DARCY
EMMA GOLDRICK
PENNY JORDAN
CAROLE MORTIMER

From top authors of Harlequin Presents comes
HARLEQUIN SUNSATIONAL, a four-stories-in-one
book with 768 pages of romantic reading.

Written by such prolific Harlequin authors as Emma Darcy,
Emma Goldrick, Penny Jordan and Carole Mortimer,
HARLEQUIN SUNSATIONAL is the perfect summer
companion to take along to the beach, cottage, on your
dream destination or just for reading at home in the warm
sunshine!

Don't miss this unique reading opportunity.

Available wherever Harlequin books are sold.

Back by Popular Demand

Janet Dailey
Americana

A romantic tour of America through fifty favorite Harlequin Presents, each set in a different state researched by Janet and her husband, Bill. A journey of a lifetime in one cherished collection.

In August, don't miss the exciting states featured in:

Title #13 — ILLINOIS
The Lyon's Share

#14 — INDIANA
The Indy Man

Available wherever Harlequin books are sold.

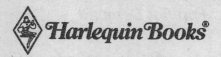 **Harlequin Books®**

GREAT NEWS...

HARLEQUIN UNVEILS NEW SHIPPING PLANS

For the convenience of customers, Harlequin has announced that Harlequin romances will now be available in stores at these convenient times each month*:

Harlequin Presents, American Romance, Historical, Intrigue:

> May titles: April 10
> June titles: May 8
> July titles: June 5
> August titles: July 10

Harlequin Romance, Superromance, Temptation, Regency Romance:

> May titles: April 24
> June titles: May 22
> July titles: June 19
> August titles: July 24

We hope this new schedule is convenient for you.

With only two trips each month to your local bookseller, you'll never miss any of your favorite authors!

*Please note: There may be slight variations in on-sale dates in your area due to differences in shipping and handling.

HDATES-RR

*Applicable to U.S. only.

Take 4 bestselling love stories FREE

Plus get a FREE surprise gift!

Special Limited-time Offer

Harlequin Reader Service®

Mail to
3010 Walden Avenue
P.O. Box 1867
Buffalo, N.Y. 14269-1867

YES! Please send me 4 free Harlequin Presents® novels and my free surprise gift. Then send me 6 brand-new novels every month, which I will receive months before they appear in bookstores. Bill me at the low price of $2.47 each—a savings of 28¢ apiece off cover prices. There are no shipping, handling or other hidden costs. I understand that accepting the books and gift places me under no obligation ever to buy any books. I can always return a shipment and cancel at any time. Even if I never buy another book from Harlequin, the 4 free books and the surprise gift are mine to keep forever.

106 BPA AC9K

Name	(PLEASE PRINT)
Address	Apt. No.
City	State	Zip

This offer is limited to one order per household and not valid to present Harlequin Presents® subscribers. Terms and prices are subject to change. Sales tax applicable in N.Y.

PRES-BPA2D   ©1990 Harlequin Enterprises Limited

This August, don't miss an exclusive
two-in-one collection of earlier love stories

MAN
WITH A PAST

TRUE COLORS

by one of today's hottest
romance authors,

Jayne Ann Krentz

Now, two of Jayne Ann Krentz's most loved books are
available together in this special edition that new and
longtime fans will want to add to their bookshelves.

Let Jayne Ann Krentz capture your hearts with the love
stories, MAN WITH A PAST and TRUE COLORS.

And in October, watch for the second two-in-one
collection by Barbara Delinsky!

Available wherever Harlequin books are sold.